TALK *Santa* TO ME

TALK

Santa
TO ME

LINDA URBAN

atheneum

NEW YORK LONDON TORONTO SYDNEY NEW DELHI

$\mathcal{A}$
atheneum

An imprint of Simon & Schuster Children's Publishing Division
1230 Avenue of the Americas, New York, New York 10020
This book is a work of fiction. Any references to historical events, real people, or real places are used fictitiously. Other names, characters, places, and events are products of the author's imagination, and any resemblance to actual events or places or persons, living or dead, is entirely coincidental.
For information about special discounts for bulk purchases, please contact Simon & Schuster Special Sales at 1-866-506-1949 or business@simonandschuster.com.
The Simon & Schuster Speakers Bureau can bring authors to your live event. For more information or to book an event, contact the Simon & Schuster Speakers Bureau at 1-866-248-3049 or visit our website at www.simonspeakers.com.
Interior design by Irene Metaxatos
The text for this book was set in ITC Veljovic Std.
Manufactured in China
First Edition
10 9 8 7 6 5 4 3 2 1
CIP data for this book is available from the Library of Congress.
ISBN 978-1-5344-7883-1 (hardcover)
ISBN 978-1-5344-7884-8 (paperback)
ISBN 978-1-5344-7885-5 (ebook)

For Claire

ORIGIN STORY

I was born in a stable. A deluxe model, indoor-outdoor stable, with a light-up roof star and grass-mat flooring (discontinued item). My mom had been carrying a three-foot shepherd from the stockroom when the first serious labor pain hit. I've always been impulsive, Mom says, and once I got the notion that I had outgrown my current quarters, boom. She knew I was moving out.

She lugged the shepherd to his spot on the showroom floor—even wholesale, indoor-outdoor shepherds are expensive; you don't drop a shepherd—and shouted for someone to call Dad. One of the before-hours stock ladies was a high school nurse making some extra money in the off-season. She got Mom to lie down among the sheep set of three and take deep, cleansing breaths in time with the music on the store sound system. Gene Autry. "Rudolph the Red-Nosed Reindeer."

"Nick!" my mom had hollered. She wanted to look into

my dad's eyes during the deep, cleansing breaths, like they had practiced in birthing class, but Dad was in the Tree Shed dealing with an artificial spruce debacle, so she focused on the polyvinyl resin face of a midsize wise man instead.

It happened fast. Rudolph had barely had a chance to go down in history before I was being swaddled in a Hollydale Holiday Shop "Christmas in July Sale" apron and nestled in her arms. Dad showed up a minute later asking if I was a boy, and could they name me Blitzen?

The story goes that my mom didn't even look at him. She just kept staring into the warm, supportive, painted-on eyes of the wise man. "Her name," she said, "is Frankincense."

Call me Francie. Please.

1

NOVEMBER 1

I am already saying I'm sorry when I fling open the door
of Uncle Jack's truck.

I'm sorry for making him wait, sorry my Santa alarm
didn't go off, sorry that even though I knew he was doing
me a special favor by picking me up at the pre-crack of
dawn on his way home from All Saints' Day Mass so I
wouldn't have to ride the freezing-cold bus to Hollydale
High School, I was not waiting on my front porch for him
as promised. Instead I had awakened fewer than five minutes earlier, when the distant rumble of his truck turning
onto Santa Claus Lane penetrated the rather excellent
dream I was having about road tripping in Uncle Jack's
pristine, vintage Miata with a teenage, pre-Wakanda
Michael B. Jordan.

From the moment I woke up, I am about to assure him, I had not dallied but had been a blur of very responsible motion, launching myself from my bed, throwing on the first-impression outfit that—thanks to the wisdom of my best friend, Alice Kim, whose smart-girl miniskirt I had borrowed as part of the ensemble—was hanging at the ready in my closet, and snagging my pre-packed backpack on the way out the door, all without whining, cursing, or turning on a single light.

It is that last bit, that dressing-in-the-dark bit, that freezes me mid-sorry, because there, in the dim cab light of Uncle Jack's pickup truck, I have suddenly come face-to-skirt with a mystery greater than the heavenly ascension of souls Uncle Jack has spent the last hour at Mass pondering.

For reasons that I cannot understand, I am not wearing Alice's smart-girl, first-impression miniskirt. What I am wearing is a puzzle. A riddle. A conundrum. It is also an insult to the spirit, a spike to the soul, and a 100% certain death blow to any hope of first-impressioning I might have planned.

What I am wearing is a knee-length, pea-green polyester skater skirt trimmed with glittering, snow-white faux fur and covered in eye-searing, electric-red candy canes.

When I say electric red, I mean electric red.

When you grow up in a family like mine, there are things you know better than most people. Which adhesive works best on a yak-hair beard, for example. Where to get a size XXXL four-inch-wide patent leather belt. How to say "Merry Christmas" in sixteen different languages. You also learn pretty quickly that though you use the word all the time, there is no such thing as *red*. There are only reds, my Grampa Chris used to say. Reds that calm and reds that alarm. Reds that make a person feel cozy and safe. Reds that stay in your vision minutes after you've closed your eyes. Crimson and vermilion and garnet and poppy and flame. Pomegranate. Merlot. Candy apple. Rose. Christmas red and Valentine red and red that looks lonely without white and blue beside it. Brick. Scarlet. Current. Blood. Plus all the reds between those colors, reds we might not even recognize as red and haven't yet been named.

So, when I say electric red, I mean *electric* red. The color of the candy canes on this ridiculous skirt in which I am inexplicably clad is electric and eye-searing and the exact opposite of the subtly sophisticated first impression I intended to make today.

Things like this do not happen to girls whose parents are accountants.

I fight my impulse to whine and curse and turn instead to beg Uncle Jack to wait just one more minute while I run inside to change. But then I notice his reaction to my outfit. A reaction that is decidedly different from mine.

Uncle Jack is crying. And not with laughter. He is legit crying. "Oh, Francie," he says, wiping his eyes. "What a beautiful gesture."

What? Am I still dreaming?

I am about to look around for Michael B. when I notice the church bulletin on the seat next to Uncle Jack, and just like that, I understand what he means. My dear, sweet Uncle Jack has interpreted this confounding wardrobe atrocity as a deliberate All Saints' Day remembrance of his father, my Grampa Chris.

I could correct him, of course, but it seems more generous to let him persist in his belief that his niece is a kind and thoughtful soul. Plus, okay, I only have about three hundred dollars in my bank account right now, and the more good feelings Uncle Jack has about me, the lower the down payment he'll probably ask when I approach him about the possibility of buying his Miata when I get my driver's license this summer. Which, if I'm perfectly honest, is already likely to be a lot lower than true market value. Uncle Jack is a softy. The oldest of his siblings and the most emotional, he tears up at hymns, coffee commercials, parades, and school plays. This is why he is a terrible Santa. As soon as a rosy-cheeked kid sits on his knee and says, "I love you," Uncle Jack starts weeping. It frightens the children.

Dad took over the Santa duties when Grampa Chris died. Other than getting totally wigged-out-nervous doing our local cable show *An Evening with Santa*, he's pretty good at it. Not as good as Grampa Chris, of course, but nobody is as good as that. In Hollydale, Christopher Wood *was* Santa Claus.

And then there's my Aunt Carole, for whom the only

explanation is a switched-at-birth hospital mix-up. Somewhere, I am certain, there is a devious Grinch family shaking their green-tinted heads over how disappointing their sweet-tempered daughter turned out to be.

"I miss him, too," I tell Uncle Jack. And it is the truth. So much the truth that I find I'm tearing up a little as well. Still, I can't go to school like this. I decide to make up some kind of story about how I wanted him to see this skirt but school is school and I'm going to run back inside and change and—

Uncle Jack takes a handkerchief from his pocket and blows his nose. "Thank you, honey," he says. Then something about his face changes. "Francie." There is a solemnity to his voice. "I understand we're running late already, but I want you to listen carefully to what I have to say and react calmly. Can you do that?"

Oh, holy night.

I suppose it was inevitable. Uncle Jack is going to tell me that despite my skirt, he is disappointed in me. That it is not okay that I was late and that I need to be more responsible. He will remind me that the Christmas season is stressful for my family and that Aunt Carole, in particular, is paying attention to my actions and that my dad is under enough pressure with the store finances and I need to tame my impulsive nature and do better. And he's right.

Go ahead, Uncle Jack. I'm ready.

"Francie." Uncle Jack takes a deep breath. "It's Lemon Square Day."

Lemon Square Day. The overhead light in the cab has dimmed, but I can still make out Uncle Jack's grin.

"Lemon . . . Square . . . Day?" I clutch my chest with one hand, grab the door handle with the other. "It's LEMON SQUARE DAY?" I pretend to swoon. Truly? You know nothing of life until you've had a lemon square from Fletcher's Bakery and Café. The sweet, tart lemon curd. The moist, cakey base. The ginger crumble topping. State secrets have been turned for such lemon squares. Marriages ruined. The confessionals at Our Lady of Sorrows Catholic Church and School have lines out the door the week of Lemon Square Day, so many selfish acts have been performed in their pursuit. And yet . . .

I am wearing a pea green skirt with electric-red candy canes on it. On the first day of a new class, first-impression day.

"What do you say?" asks Uncle Jack.

What *do* I say?

Impulse or impression?

Confection or costume change?

Dessert or dignity?

2

The ginger crumble of a Fletcher's Bakery lemon square is covered with an obscene amount of powdered sugar, and now, after a bumpy ride in Uncle Jack's pickup truck, so am I. There's no time to do much about it except button my cardigan across my chest, hold my binder low over the front of my skirt, and dart into Mythology Today as the bell rings. Mythology Today is one of these quarter-long exploratory English classes that Hollydale feels "brings relevance and authenticity to student reading and writing." With our block schedule, that means I'll have it Tuesdays, Thursdays, and alternating Fridays—barring holidays, make-up sessions, and principal caprice.

A glance confirms what I expected: There are a few sophomores in the class, but most are juniors. Cluster of comic book and theater kids. Pack of puckheads in the back. All in all, a pretty random sampling of the Hollydale student body. I slip into the closest available desk, open my binder in my lap so it covers most of my skirt, and try to convince myself of the unlikelihood that anyone would notice anyway, or care. Yesterday was Halloween, after all, and last week some of these people wore vampire teeth and full-on Wookies suits to school.

I try to focus. At the front of the room, Ms. Colando is leaning on a lectern, fiddling with her class list. I don't know much about her except that she goes to Comic-Con every July, where, apparently, she spends as much money on official T-shirts as she does hotel and airfare. There exists at Hollydale High School a much-agreed-upon rumor that Ms. Colando once had an evening of unspeakable Comic-Con romance with one of the guys who played Batman, though there is no consensus as to whether it was with Affleck or Keaton. Some even espouse an Adam West theory, but those people do so more for the entertainment value of the claim than any real faith in the position.

Today Ms. Colando has selected a vintage T-shirt from 2004. The shirt has faded to a dead-mothy color but the central image remains discernable—a particularly biceptual Superman flexing himself free of the sort of chain my best friend, Alice, and I once used to lock our bikes to the rack outside the public library. As Ms. Colando starts talking, I wonder how Superman got himself into this be-chained state. What sort of villain would employ such pathetic restraints? Maybe a super-pumped Tour de France–type. The Cyclist? No, wait . . . the Doper. Stripped of his glory after a steroid investigation, the Doper vows revenge against the firecracker reporter who broke the story, Superman's main squeeze, Lois Lane. The Doper has captured Lois, dressed her in unflattering spandex, and locked her in his parents' garage, where he threatens to . . . do something. My story stalls here, as they often do. This is why I took Mythology Today this quarter instead of Creative Writing. I've got a knack for setup, but after that it takes more faith in the story's outcome than I am able to muster. Seems smarter to stick with writing about things I know.

"Frankincense?" asks Ms. Colando.

I look up, afraid that I have been caught daydreaming and ruined my first impression already, but Ms. Colando is not looking at me. She has her finger on her attendance book. My inattentiveness has not caught her eye; my name has.

There is the usual snickering from the room. A few people have been in class with me before, but since I never use it, they've forgotten my full name. For everyone else, my name is new and an opportunity for momentary mockery. "Frankincense," repeats one of the puckheads in a voice that is both goofy and vaguely threatening.

"Francie," I tell Ms. Colando.

"Francie." Ms. Colando makes eye contact, scratches

something into her attendance book, then points her pencil at me. "What is myth?"

Despite my Superman daydreaming, I have been paying enough attention to know this is not the only time she has asked the question this period. She's one of those teachers who swears there is no right answer and therefore asks the same question over and over, soliciting a broad variety of responses. Of course, there is a right answer, which you know because these same teachers quit asking the question once they have received it. Apparently we have not yet reached that point.

Most of the answers thus far have been about gods and goddesses. DeKieser Shelby covered the "ancient" angle and also said something about explanatory stories. Of course she didn't use that exact vocabulary. She said "old, old stories or whatever where the people tried to figure out stuff?" DeKieser's really smart and particularly good at math—something I never would have guessed when we first met because of the way she talks. Now that we're friends, I've learned to think of her use of words like *"stuff"* and *"whatever"* as variables like x or y—placeholders for real words, which, through a logical, systematic process, are actually deducible. Unfortunately, just as many of my high school peers avoid higher math, concluding that it is too hard, they also avoid DeKieser, concluding that she is too simple. DeKieser says she doesn't care, though. That her real friends and the girls she dates understand what she means and that's enough. Like I said, DeKieser is really smart.

Ms. Colando waits as I grasp for another definition of myth. "Things people believe that really aren't true," I say. Several rows behind me, there's a strangulated cough, like someone has inhaled a wad of chewing gum. Laughter follows.

"Mm-hmm," says Ms. Colando. She marks her book, then scans the room for another answer. I will need to pay better attention in this class. No more supervillain daydreams. At least, not until I figure Ms. Colando out enough to know what sort of answers she does want. Soul-searching and abstract? I can meet that challenge. Brief and factual? I can do that too. Parroting her own words? Easy-peasy. I went to Catholic school for nine years before coming to Hollydale last year.

"What is myth?" Ms. Colando consults her attendance book again. "Gunther?"

Gunther Hobbes. First-string defenseman. Varsity hockey. Apparently he was in the pack of puckheads I glimpsed earlier. I tuck my skirt further under my binder.

"Myth is what you have to study if Sports Writing is full," says Gunther. The puckheads crack up again.

"You can write about sports in this class if you choose," says Ms. Colando. "Aside from contemporary religions, you can write about practically any subject that has a mythology to it."

"Why can't we write about religion?" asks a theater girl.

"Because I'd like to keep my job," says Ms. Colando.

"There's no mythology in hockey," says someone else in the puckhead region of the classroom.

"Ah, but there's a mythology *of* hockey." Ms. Colando taps the lectern. "I'm not really equipped to tell you about it, since I don't know much about the game—"

"All you have to know is Vikings RULE!" The puckheads make loud hooting sounds and slap their desks.

Ms. Colando is neither amused nor irritated—or at least, she *looks* neither amused nor irritated. She looks like someone waiting for elevator doors to open, like she understands the futility of anything other than patient endurance.

Another voice: "Myth is a way of keeping order. It's how people in power tell a story confirming that things are exactly the way they should be."

Even before I turn around I know what happened. Some poor nerd came to class early and sat in a seemingly safe spot near the back of the room, only to be surrounded by a pack of late-arriving puckheads. A single salmon among grizzlies.

I turn to look as best I can without disturbing the binder on my lap, but find the back quarter of the room salmon-free.

"And people not in power?" asks Ms. Colando.

"Myths tell them that whatever lousy situation they're in is either fate or their fault. It keeps them from trying to do something about it."

The speaker is no fish. He is Hector Ramirez. Recent transfer student. Sophomore. He's in the same Algebra II class that DeKieser and I are in. I would have recognized him if he'd been sitting a few rows in front of me, as he does in Algebra II. He has noteworthy shoulders, Hector Ramirez does. I can say this objectively.

It turns out his shoulders are equally nice from the front. I draw this conclusion just as someone from behind Hector's noteworthy shoulders offers a roundhouse slug to his arm, knocking him a few inches sideways. A few inches is all that is necessary to reveal the dimpled face of the slugger. Sam Spinek.

Oh, holy night.

Ms. Colando is talking again and people around me seem to be writing something down, but for a second I swear I smell chlorine and it's hard to think. Eventually, the bell rings. I tuck my skirt more tightly under myself and make a show of zipping up a pencil case so I can stay seated until the puckheads leave. They do so in a clump, bumping shoulders and hooting. I wait until it's just me and DeKieser in the room before lifting my binder from my lap and getting up out of my seat. Which is how I'm caught standing in front of my desk, electric candy canery in full view, as first-string defenseman Gunther Hobbes leans back into the classroom.

"Nice outfit," he says. And then he sticks out his tongue.

"Ew," says DeKieser when Gunther returns, hooting, to

3

TWO YEARS AGO . . .

This is how it happened. I was a few weeks shy of my thir-
teenth birthday and was sitting with Mina Patel on her
front porch. Mina is a year older than I am and lives in
the small subdivision behind the Hollydale Holiday Shop,
making her one of the few friends whose houses I could
walk to. Even so, we were just summer friends, together
only when Alice was in Michigan visiting her Korean
grandma and Mina couldn't get her brother to drive her to
her real friends' houses. We hung out as middle schoolers
must, fully aware that if either of us had other options,
we'd take them.

Anyway, we were sitting there talking about all the
places we'd drive to if we had cars and licenses when Sam
Spinek came riding by on his bike. Mina and I had hung

out with him a couple times earlier that week, once even talking about the origins of our names (Sam, named for the one-time governor of Texas; Mina, named for the daughter of a Hindu god and also of a distant aunt; me, well, you know the story). Sam was fourteen then, like Mina, and went to public school like Mina, and played hockey like Mina, and so when he stopped in front of the house, he and Mina talked about all those things for a while.

Sam Spinek has this scar under his right eye that he got from a hockey puck. The scar looks like a dimple, and as he and Mina talked, I watched it move. I watched it and I watched it until I was mesmerized by it. Until I came to the conclusion that I could keep on watching it until the end of time, which reminded me to check my phone. It was eight o'clock and I had promised Mom I'd be home by eight thirty, so I told Mina goodbye and started walking. I was only a few houses away when Sam Spinek and his mesmerizing dimple rode up beside me. "Hey, Frankincense," he said. "I can give you a ride if you want."

Oh, dimpled boy, I thought. *I want.*

Without another thought, I got on his bike, and he started doing that standing-up-to-pedal thing you have to do when someone else is sitting on your bike and I had to hold on to his hips so I wouldn't fall, which was pretty mesmerizing in its own right. And then Sam Spinek stand-pedaled me out of Mina's subdivision and down Fair Street and up Santa Claus Lane and to the bottom of my driveway. I got off his bike and I whispered thanks and there was this strange blankety quiet between us. Sam Spinek was still straddling his bike and his hands were still on the handlebars but his face started getting closer to mine, and then there was nothing but face and dimple, and just like that I knew he was going to kiss me.

This gorgeous, dimpled older boy was going to kiss *me*. My first kiss.

I closed my eyes in anticipation of his lips.

What I felt was not really lips so much as tongue pushing into my mouth—stiff and straight, like one of those balsa wood sticks at the pediatrician's office.

What's the word for that stick? I remember thinking. And then, *Why is this tongue in my mouth?*

It is French kissing, I told myself.

The French are messed up, myself told me. *But we're kissing, right? This is kissing?*

And then Sam Spinek took his tongue out of my mouth and I said goodbye and he pedaled away and I walked up the long driveway to my house. I must have opened the door because I was inside the house. And I must have gone up the stairs because then I was in my room. And I must have walked to the window because then I was looking outside and I was not seeing Sam Spinek or his bicycle but I was thinking, *I have been kissed. I have had my first kiss.* And suddenly all the parts of my nearly thirteen-year-old body react. Face sees how many capillaries it can fire off at one time. Stomach does an inventory of its contents and considers ridding itself of them all. Knees make like bendy straws. Hair prickles at nape. Tongue? Tongue is unresponsive. Just as it had been earlier. But now it wonders, *Should I have moved or something?*

The answer came a few days later in Mina's backyard swimming pool. There was swimming. There was splashing. There was Marco Polo–ing. I, feeling worldly now that I had had someone else's tongue in my mouth, teased Mina's brother, Amar, who was a junior and very popular. He and his friends would not have chosen to share this body of water with me under any other circumstances but that Mina invited me in and it was 92 degrees out.

I've forgotten now what I said to Amar, but I know what he said in response: "Oh yeah?" That, I remember quite well. Amar said, "Oh yeah?" and then he said, "At least I know how to kiss."

Tongue was supposed to do something!

"Did you kiss Francie?" Mina yelled at Amar.

"Heck, no. Spinek did. He said she doesn't know how to kiss. He told us at Weights."

"Weights" is what Amar called the Patel family garage where he had a bunch of barbells and a bench and some other workout stuff, and where he and his fellow cool boys could lift and grunt and, apparently, swap stories about neighbor girls and their lack of kissing acumen.

I sunk underwater. If Amar had more to say, I didn't want to hear it. Through the chlorinated blue, I could see the bottom half of Mina, slim in her bikini. Amar's leg hair was thick enough to be noticed from across the pool. Marco and the Polos were still. I stayed there, submerged, trying to think of what I could say when I surfaced. I could think of nothing. Nothing. Nothing. What seemed like minutes passed. Less and less air reached my brain. Even now, I swear I saw an octopus swim by.

"Even I know how to kiss," the possible octopus said as he passed. "Your life is over."

My lungs chimed in that the octopus would be right unless I surfaced, and so I did. People were Marco Polo-ing again, but their hearts were not in it. They were only pretending to search for one another. Mina had threatened them and said they would all have to get out of the pool and go home if anyone said another word, but Amar was done swimming anyway. He pulled himself up out of the water in such a manly way one would have suspected he had been paid to do so by a swimsuit company. "I'm going to lift," he told his friends, who upon hearing this declaration leaped from the water like theme park seals. I watched them towel off and follow him to Weights, then turn momentarily toward me, as if directed by some hidden force, and in unison, stick out their popular-boy tongues.

A depressor, I remembered then. That's what it's called.

4

I'm still thinking about Gunther Hobbes's tongue when the bus drops me off at the North Pole. Santa Claus Lane is a private road, about a half mile long. Near the far end, on the eastern side, it sprouts a long driveway, which leads up a small rise to my family's house. Colonial-style, built in the 1970s, it looks exactly the same as the colonials that elbow one another in the tight subdivisions that surround the old-town part of Hollydale. Our house is notable only for the fact that there are no other such houses in view here. What is in view is the Hollydale Holiday Shop, which sits on the opposite side of Santa Claus Lane.

The Holiday Shop is not a single storefront but a collection of buildings that were once part of a small nineteenth-century dairy operation. A midsize milking barn is now a two-story retail space, the majority of which is stocked year-round with Christmas decor. The front display area changes seasonally, depending on the profitability of the holiday. St. Patrick's is hardly worth putting shamrocks out for, but Halloween is money. If this wasn't an Alice day, Mom would have me working in the shop right now, moving the skeletons and zombie masks to the discount bins and replacing them with hand-painted turkey platters and LET'S GIVE THANKS yard signs. When I got home from school, I peeked in long enough to see that the day's display transition had been slow. The Día de los Muertos display looked fairly picked over, while the front table featured both pilgrims and vampires. Norman Rockwell, meet Norman Bates.

On the far side of the barn, nearest the parking lot, is the Tree Shed, the interior of which looks like Walt Disney fever-dreamed a forest. Grampa Chris used to love this building. Noble fir, spruce, Norwegian pine, balsam—all artificial, all pre-lit, all thematically decorated ("Baby's First Christmas," "Visions of Sugar Plums," "Mele Kalikimaka")—line a wandering path edged by a six-inch-tall picket fence and blankets of glitter-spattered Faux Snow. Tucked between the trees are some of our best automatons: Santa at his desk scribbling a Nice list; Mrs. Claus obsessively huffing out a candle; an elf removing a shiny green present from Santa's pack, thinking better of the gift, and shoving it back into the bag. We don't sell a lot of these, but they are a big draw for families. Kids love the magic of watching something move, wondering if some tiny part of that elf or Claus is alive. You can see the kids completely transfixed, holding their breath in the possibility. They wait for the mechanical Santa to reveal his aliveness—to wink or whisper the watcher's name—to say *Yes, I am real and you, special child, are the only one who knows.* At least, I assume this is still true. I don't really go in the Tree Shed anymore.

The Tree Shed eats up a lot of electricity, so we don't open it until the first weekend of November, which is this upcoming weekend, which is why, as I stand at the bus stop in front of the North Pole texting Alice, I can sometimes hear my dad shouting for someone to check the wheels on the Gumdrop Express or to turn the flocker on a Frasier fir.

There are a couple of other outbuildings around, mostly for storage. A five-car garage houses the trailer-mounted sled and mechanical reindeer we use for the Hollydale Holiday Parade, as well as the true miracle of vehicles, Uncle Jack's beautiful, yellow, tarp-covered Miata. Unlike the Tree Shed, I visit the garage whenever I can.

Aside from the shop itself, the building I spend the most time in is the administrative building for the Holiday Shop business, a building we call the North Pole. Once upon a time, the North Pole was a sprawling old farmhouse where my Grampa Chris spent his childhood, but when he took over the ornament-import business from his father, he converted the farmhouse into administrative offices, the staff breakroom, and, eventually, Santa School classrooms. It's the marketing face of the business. The image on every Santa School brochure and tourist flyer we print.

When Uncle Jack and I drove to school this morning, the North Pole was still decorated for Halloween, but sometime during the day the window ghosts and jack-o'-lanterns were replaced with our traditional Christmas fare. For as long as I can remember, the North Pole has been tastefully decorated, with tiny white lights on the roofline ($9.99 per one hundred–bulb strand) and an artificial boxwood wreath in each of the nine front windows, illuminated by an electric candle and tied with a crimson bow. Traditionally, the front door has been similarly be-wreathed, but this year, after a significant argument, Aunt Carole convinced Dad to let her robotic intern, Bryan, replace the artificial boxwood with a massive modern silver job, barnacled with mirrored bulbs and chunky crystals. This is my first up close look at it. It looks like somebody hot glued a snow tire with rhinestones and foil-wrapped potatoes.

I drop my backpack on the porch and sit underneath the wreath, tucking my ridiculous skirt under my legs to protect me from the scratchy SEASON'S GREETINGS doormat ($54.95). It is possible that DeKieser was right, that Gunther was simply responding to the candy canes on my skirt or even to the powdered sugar on my sweater. The taunting of my thirteenth summer did not last long, after all. Utter humiliation prevented me from ever going back to Mina's house. Occasionally during the following few weeks I'd be with Mom at the grocery store or walking across Fair Street to go to the library and some boy would stick his tongue out at me. But then Grampa Chris died and so, too, did the teasing. At least, I thought it did.

When Alice's bus gets here, I'll tell her what happened and she'll use all her investigative reporter skills to sort it out for me. I find myself wondering for the billionth time if I should have just continued my Catholic education and gone to Regina, Queen of Heaven like Alice did. Then we'd be at the same school, where there'd be no Sam Spinek and no Gunther Hobbes, and if somehow there was a Gunther Hobbes–like person around, Alice would dig up some dirt on them and threaten to print it in the school paper and that would be that.

For a second, I worry that I got the day wrong, that Alice has newspaper after school today. Or that she's decided that it is just too hard to keep a friendship going this way. That it is more convenient to hang out with Regina girls or friends who live within walking distance of her house. Next year, when I can drive, it will be easier. I'll pick Alice up after school and we won't be stuck doing homework at my house with my brothers in our business and Mom calling to remind me to remind Gram to put the lasagna in the oven. If I still believed in Santa, that's what I'd put on my list. I'd also ask him to make sure Alice doesn't get too fed up with our situation before I get my license and buy Uncle Jack's Miata. Maybe I'd ask for the money to buy it too.

I did start texting Alice about what happened with Gunther, but since I seem to lack the basic skill that typifies my generation, nearly every text I send requires dedicated proofreading or NSA-level decoding. After a few autocorrect mishaps, I give up. Alice isn't answering, anyway, which means she's probably busy talking with one of her Regina friends, or maybe even flirting with a guy. In a cost-saving measure, Alice's school shares buses with the Catholic boys' high school, Saint Lawrence, and a nearby academy for teenage Protestants. Apparently this makes the bus a sort of interfaith club scene for teens who can't yet drive.

From inside the North Pole I can hear Aunt Carole's voice, which is the exact pitch and timbre to rattle the wreath above my head. A moment later, the door clicks open behind me. Intern Bryan.

"Francesca," she says in a way that is both chirpy and clipped and which only strengthens my suspicion that Bryan is not really the community college business student she claims to be but a robot Aunt Carole has been constructing on weekends.

"Briana," I say. If she can get my name wrong, I can at least return the favor. I see her soulless eyes fixate on the candy-caned abomination I'm wearing and I prepare myself for a snide robotic remark.

"Where's the vest?" she says.

If that's a joke, I'm not getting it. "What vest?"

"The vest that goes with the skirt. Carole had me hang it in your closet so you couldn't claim to have misplaced it."

I can't believe this. "You went in my closet? In my room? In my house?"

Bryan squints. That might not seem like a smug gesture, but it is. "There was a complete set of instructions pinned to the garment. The skirt and vest are a uniform sample. You're to wear it for a week and report back with your impressions."

"I can report back right now. It's hideous."

Squint. "If you had read the instructions, you would have seen that aesthetic evaluations will be left up to customer focus groups. You are to provide data on durability, breathability, cleanability, visibility, and any significant restriction of movement."

"This was all on your note?"

"I'm very thorough," she says, patting her notebook.

For two years, I have told everyone—Mom, Dad, Alice, anyone who asks—that the reason I chose to go to Hollydale High instead of Regina like so many of my Catholic school peers was the uniforms. Every day, the same thing. Plaid skirt, white blouse, green cardigan, green knee socks. No buttons, pins, or noticeable adornments. Each girl in the school was expected to look as much as possible like the next. I swear if they could have issued us identical wigs, they would have. And now Aunt Carole wants uniforms at the shop? I have to believe this is a personal attack, but it would be a huge investment for the store to dress every employee in eye-blistering elf-wear just to torment me. "What does everyone else think?" I ask Bryan.

"Carole is excited about the opportunity to maximize the *experiential nature* of the Hollydale Holiday Shop. The right uniform, she believes, will boost—"

"I'm not talking about Aunt Carole. I mean the rest of the staff. The cashiers. Receiving. The ladies in Invitations. I can't see Dottie rocking a vest."

A tight little grin from Bryan. "This is a *sample* uniform, Francesca. *You* are trying it out first."

It *is* a personal attack! "No," I say. "No way. I'm not walking around the shop like some deranged elf while everyone else looks normal."

"Deranged would reflect your demeanor more than it would the uniform. No, no. Colorful! Playful! Welcoming! Smile-making! Those are the terms more in keeping with the brand identity we're after." Bryan pauses and tilts her head, as if she is waiting for further instructions to be radioed from headquarters. They must arrive, because a second later she is tearing a page from her notebook and holding it out to me with a stiff robot arm.

"What's this?" I ask, but I don't need to. The page is clearly labeled: *TO-DO LIST FOR F.* Underneath, in mechanical-looking print, are three items:

EXPERIENCE UNIFORM

COPY MANUAL AND MAIL TO SANTA FRANKLIN

COMPLETE UNIFORM EVALUATION SHEET BY

SATURDAY MORNING

I hold the list out for her to take back. "Check the schedule,. Bry. I don't work today."

"But you're wearing your uniform."

"I didn't know it was a uniform."

"So, you *chose* the deranged-elf look of your own free will?"

I am not explaining to Bryan about dressing in the dark. "Yesterday was Halloween and I agreed to give out candy at the shop so I could have this afternoon off instead, so you can take your list back." I'm not working today. I'm not doing her list. I am hanging out with Alice. Alice and I only get to see each other a couple of times a week and I am not giving up one of them just so that Bryan can impress Aunt Carole with her personnel management skills.

"Dear, dear." Bryan flips open her notebook again. "Carole will be so disappointed. Initiative and Dedication are two of the Pillars of Employee Excellence." Her pen hovers a few inches above what I know is my probation page. A week after Grampa Chris died, Aunt Carole moved here from California to "help out," which meant bringing a whole bunch of new ideas for how the shop could be modernized and improved. Dad has fought off most of her changes, but he gives her a little territory now and again to keep her off his back. The silver door wreath was one such concession. Another was letting her implement a probationary period for all new hires, during which time there are points for things she calls Pillars: Attendance, Customer Service, Initiative, Holiday Spirit, and the rest. After you work ninety days and get enough points for all the Pillars of Excellence, you qualify for certain benefits, start accruing vacation days, and, most important, get a raise "commensurate with your Pillar level." In short, Aunt Carole controls how fast I get my Miata money.

"But I don't work today," I say again. I hate how I sound. Pleading with Bryan is as pathetic as begging an ATM to front you a few bucks. As effective, too. Bryan shrugs and lowers her pen to the paper.

"Wait! Okay. I'm already wearing this stupid skirt. I'll keep experiencing it," I say.

"And Santa Franklin?"

"I'll send him the manual materials. After dinner, okay? I won't be in anyone's way if I use the copier then. All the staff will be gone." *Okay, Bryan? Okay?* I hate myself.

Bryan caps her pen and I swear I hear the *ping!* of an application shutting down. "That's the Holiday Spirit!" she chirps. The North Pole door closes. My wreath reflection shudders. Or maybe that's just me.

5

9 check my phone.

3:30.

3:32.

Where are you? I text Alice.

This time she replies. **Bus driver George stopped to lecture some hooligans from Trinity.**

Lute hens lack discipline. *Dang.* **Lutherans.** I wait for Alice to emoji a cry-laugh at my mistake, but the phone is silent. I could take out my algebra book and get some homework done, but instead I watch a couple of little girls bicycling on the patio outside the public library across the street. Strings of lights stretch high above them, hung in anticipation of the fundraising tree lot that will open Thanksgiving week. The lights are a good ten feet above their heads, but the girls raise their hands as they ride, like they believe they can stretch to touch them.

Finally, Alice's bus pulls up to the traffic light at the intersection of Fair Street and Hill. I grab my backpack and step off the porch even though it takes another two minutes for the bus to make the turn onto Fair and rumble to a stop in front of the North Pole. It's a warm-enough afternoon that the bus windows are down. I hear Alice's Regina friends call out their goodbyes.

"What does this mean?" Alice de-buses, holding her phone out so I can see my texts. "'Sample neck'?"

The bus belches, then rumbles away.

"Sam Spinek," I clarify.

She swipes her screen. "'Misogyny today'?"

"Mythology. Sam Spinek is in my mythology class." We start up Santa Claus Lane toward my house. I walk slowly, knowing this is our only chance for a real, private conversation. Once we get inside, Gram and my brothers will be around. Gram gives us our privacy, but Don and Dash are spies. Add that to the Why I Need the Miata list. Privacy.

I tell Alice about Mythology Today and Sam and Gunther. I don't even notice right away that she has steered us away from my house, through the shop parking lot, and around to the back entrance of the North Pole. "We need a Cookie Council," she says, nudging me toward the kitchen-turned-staff-breakroom door. My grandmother has little to do with the running of the store anymore, but she continues her daily commitment to filling the breakroom cookie jar with treats for the employees. To be honest, Alice will call a Cookie Council over just about anything, but this time I agree that it is warranted.

We reach the North Pole breakroom as one of the new seasonal employees from Outdoor Decor is leaving. "Such a darling skirt," she tells me on her way out the door. "I'd wear something like that if I could get away with it."

Get away with it. Like wearing an unflattering garment is equivalent to bank robbery or auto theft. *Here's the plan, see? I'm gonna put on this T-shirt. It's gonna make my boobs look droopy, so have the getaway car ready!*

"Sit," Alice tells me. She lifts the head off the snowman cookie jar and peeks inside. "Molasses!"

"So, Sam Spinek—" I say.

Alice holds up a hand. "Cookies first. You know Council procedure." She takes a chipped "For the Big Guy" ($14.99) plate from the cupboard, arranges four molasses cookies on it, and recapitates the snowman. "*Elf in Training* or wreath?" she asks, reaching for a coffee mug.

"A pox upon the elves."

Alice grabs the wreath mug for me and selects a black "Coal Collector" mug for herself. She pours us each a cup of coffee before discovering that there is no sugar left in the sugar bowl. Neither of us drink our coffee black, but since it is protocol, she brings the mugs to the table anyway. When we're both seated, coffee in hand, plate of cookies between us, Alice begins.

"So, how did this happen? You've been at that school

for over a year without a single tongue-related incident of any kind."

"Of any kind." I put on my beleaguered no-boy-thinks-I'm-dateable act but Alice knows me well and lets the comment pass.

"Is this really the first time you've seen him? This Sam guy?"

"The whole teasing thing only lasted a few weeks that summer," I remind her. She was in Michigan visiting her halmoni the whole time and only came home for Grampa Chris's funeral. "And I was at Sorrows for a year before I went to Hollydale. I must have passed Sam in the hallway a hundred times as a freshman, but he never said anything. He probably didn't even recognize me." I look a lot different than I did at nearly thirteen. My hair is shorter and darker than it was, and wearing a bra is no longer an aspirational act. I'm five inches taller and several inches wider in places that still surprise me. "This is the first time we've had a class together," I add.

"Hmm," says Alice. "Thus, for an entire freshman year you walked the halls of Hollydale in obscurity—" I notice an Australian accent creeping into Alice's voice as it does when she is feeling particularly clever. She and her Regina crew have Acorn subscriptions and have become big fans of *Miss Fisher's Murder Mysteries*.

"I have friends," I say.

"—a relative unknown. Invisible. Unremarked upon."

"There have been remarks—"

"But none from upperclassmen. None from those particular boys, right?"

"Right," I admit.

"Until today, when they heard your name. Your unforgettable name."

I dunk a molasses cookie into my coffee, thinking maybe it will sweeten the drink. It doesn't. A nibble proves I've ruined the cookie, too.

"I've embittered it." I drop the cookie on the plate. Alice nabs it, undeterred.

"And then you implied that myth is a lie. A LIE, Francie."

"So? It kind of is."

"As was Mr. Spinek's claim that you did not know how to kiss."

"That wasn't a lie. I didn't know how to kiss," I say. I *don't*.

"But you now know, through extensive reading and movie watching if not through actual in-the-field experience, that Mr. Spinek did not possess that skill at the time either," says Alice. *Eigh-tha. Mistah.* She's deep into her Miss Fisher–speak now.

"Nobody else knows that."

"PRECISELY!" Alice leaps to her feet. "Mr. Spinek spun the myth his way—Francie Wood doesn't know how to kiss—and he relied on the resulting mortification to keep you quiet. But then—THEN"—she leaps again—"you, in your first class together, say . . . what did you say? A story people take as fact but that isn't true? Which is the same as a LIE, which is the same, my dear Francie, as threatening to out Mr. Spinek as one unschooled in the kissing arts."

"He seems pretty schooled now." I've seen him making out in the hallway with several girls. Not all at the same time, of course, but in fairly rapid succession.

"All the more reason to protect his past, right?" The *right* has slipped from Miss Fisher territory into that chimney guy from *Mary Poppins*. "So, he offers a subtle reminder of your—"

"Humiliation."

"—to his cronies, and Bob's your uncle."

"Jack's my uncle," I say, but I know what she means— simple as that, Sam restored the memory of that summer to his puckhead friends and gave Gunther permission to tease me about it.

"So what do I do?" I ask.

She shrugs and polishes off the last bite of cookie. "Give me a minute to think. By the way, what happened here?" She lifts her coffee mug in the direction of my skirt and raises an eyebrow. Eyebrow communication is apparently important in *Miss Fisher* and Alice is determined to master it.

I explain about the uniforms. "Another of Carole's evil schemes for Holiday Spirit and World Domination."

"Devious," she says, maybe about Aunt Carole, though possibly about the coffee. "Thirty more workdays, right?"

"Twenty-nine." Even though I've been helping at the shop since I was three (somebody has to tinsel the trees),

I couldn't become a payroll employee with a real work schedule and time card until I turned fifteen. Since I wanted my summer free to hang with Alice as much as possible, I waited to officially begin working until after school started.

"This is abuse," says Alice. "Hey, wait . . . this is *abuse*! That's a good idea for a story, isn't it? The exploitation of underage workers by heartless capitalist fat cats. Now there's a story the *Daily* would have to print!" Alice is determined to get a story published in the local paper before she graduates. "Can I interview you?" she asks.

"The fat cats are my parents, Alice. And they aren't that fat." In fact, money has been kind of tight at the shop. The stress and extra work hours have made Mom and Dad both lose weight in the two years since they took over the business, enough that Dad has had to order two sequentially smaller Santa suits and three sequentially larger fake bellies ($64.50).

"Right. Okay." Alice's eyebrows furrow as she takes another sip of coffee.

"You don't have to drink that," I remind her.

"It helps me think," she says. "And now that I have thought, I have your answer: You, Frankincense Wood, need a boyfriend."

"You're not kidding," I say, bringing back the no-boy-will-ever-be-interested-in-me shtick.

"And you need to engage in some conspicuous PDA. Sam Spinek and his buds will see you hot and heavy in the Hollydale halls and they will have nothing left to tease you about."

"Uh-huh. And where is this boyfriend supposed to come from? You forget that not a single boy has asked me out since Peter Pontaski in seventh grade."

"Peter moved to Florida, didn't he? Tough luck. He might have been a good target." Alice takes another swig of thinking juice, apparently stumped by the lack of possibilities. "I could set you up with a Saint Lawrence boy, but it wouldn't help with the PDA. You'll have to ask someone out yourself. Isn't there anyone at Hollydale you'd like to kiss?"

Several names float to mind, including Michael B. Jordan, who—of course—does not go to Hollydale, and the fine-shouldered Hector Ramirez, who does, but who, frankly, is no more real a possibility given that (1) I barely know him, (2) he barely knows me, and (3) Alice's plan stinks. "No," I say.

"Uh-huh." Alice tries another eyebrow raise. I'm grateful when a sip of coffee wipes the knowing look from her face.

She's probably right. Gunther and his pals will probably forget about all of this by tomorrow, and if they don't, some Hollydale hallway make out action could do the trick. But I don't have a boyfriend. And I don't want one. Because if I had one, I'd have to kiss him, which, rather than correcting everyone's impression, might just confirm it.

6

NOVEMBER 2

Five forty-five a.m. My alarm, which did not go off yesterday morning when I needed it to, now *ho ho ho*s from my desk across the room. It's a Santa-in-the-Chimney alarm clock, plucked from last year's bargain bin by my mother after I kept letting my phone battery die. When the chimney alarm goes off, a light-up Santa pops up and *ho*s for sixty seconds, and if you don't turn him off he'll sing "Jingle Bell Rock" at you.

I beat the song by a second, but Santa's still glowing enough that I can see my uniform vest hanging in the closet, the note Bryan wrote still attached. I probably should have read it last night, but after Alice's dad picked her up and I ate dinner and did homework and tried to distract myself from thinking about Alice's PDA plan by watching a bootleg YouTube episode of *Miss Fisher* so I could see what she and her friends are on about, I fell asleep.

Dang! I forgot to copy the manual for Santa Franklin last night!

I flick on the lights, throw on the first nonholiday–themed clothes I find, and quietly hurl myself downstairs. Dad hangs his keys on a hook by the door—not just the house keys but keys for the shop and the Tree Shed and the storage garage and the North Pole. For the first time in ages, I am grateful that we live across the street from the shop. I can borrow the keys, dash over to the North Pole, make my copies, return the keys, and no one will be the wiser.

It's quiet in Hollydale at six a.m. There are only a few cars on Fair Street and we don't turn on the Christmas music in the parking lot until the store opens at nine. I can hear my feet on the pavement. My breath. The parking lot lights are dimmed, but the string lights on the shop and the North Pole are bright and pure-looking, and even though I know that Jerry and Tom from Receiving spent the last two weekends replacing every burned-out bulb, I can also almost believe that the lights are really Christmas fairies lured by the holiday spirit of the place—just like Grampa Chris used to say.

Inside the North Pole I actually remember the code to turn off the alarm system and find the emergency flashlight we keep mounted underneath it. My parents are still nestled snug in their bed, but if they did wake up and see a light on over here, they'd probably call the security company to investigate. I point the flashlight at the floor and make my way to Snowflake, the largest of the three Santa School rooms.

Unlike the other two classrooms which were once front and back parlors, Snowflake is a recent addition to the building. When Grampa Chris started the school he had only a half-dozen students, and even though Santas tend to be pretty plump, we could get them all into what had been the front parlor and still have enough room to demonstrate proper parade waving. About ten years ago, though, the number of Santa students grew, plus we started getting applications from women who wanted Ms. Santa training—not to mention the occasional over-enthusiastic elf who promised that if we let them into this year's class we'd all have a jingling good time!

Grampa Chris never wanted to exclude anyone, so he took out a sizable loan and built Snowflake. It's my favorite room, and when I was little I was sure that Santa's own living room must have looked exactly the same. A fireplace and ceiling beams and mullioned windows and a wall of glass-fronted shelves filled with hundreds of books about Santa and Christmas and holiday traditions. The shelves sit on top of cupboards and oak file cabinets with records of all the students who have come to the school. I find the master copy of the manual in one of those files and take it upstairs to the accounting office copy machine.

The Santa School manual is about 150 pages long, front

and back, and it serves as the textbook for the Hollydale Holiday Shop Santa School. It's got tips on wardrobe and etiquette and vocal conditioning. There's some media guidance for television appearances, like the *An Evening with Santa* show that freaks Dad out so much, along with sheet music for Christmas carols and a long section about Christmas lore and how the holiday is celebrated in different countries. Most of the manual was written by Grampa Chris when he founded the school, and aside from updating the sample employment contracts and changing the date on the front page, I don't think anyone has revised it in a long time. The Santas—especially the repeat students like Santa Franklin—love having it, just like they love their graduation suspenders and their commemorative sleigh bells. When a freak October storm flooded Santa Franklin's basement, the first person he called was Dad so he could get a replacement. Only after that was settled did he call his insurance agent.

While the pages are double-siding themselves through the copier, I flashlight my way to a mailing envelope and print on it the address I got from Santa Franklin's student file. The last of the pages *shuszh* through the machine and the copier settles into a self-satisfied hum. I'm feeling pretty satisfied with myself too. All I have to do is pop the copies into the envelope and drop them in the outgoing mail bin. No one will ever have to know I messed up, I'll get my Pillar Points, and I can keep my sunshine-yellow Miata dream alive.

I look down at the copies resting in their tray and am surprised to see a photo of a Santa looking back, a he-sees-you-when-you're-sleeping look on his face. It is not the Big Brotherness of this surveillance Santa that surprises me. It's the Santa himself. The photo is not of my dad. It's not of Grampa Chris, either. It could be one of the student Santas from the past few years, but even though he looks familiar, my brain is not settling on that connection. The photo is of a fairly fit-looking Santa (as Santas go) and unlike the picture cards and department store shots we see from most of our graduates, this one is perfectly lit. There's a sparkle in the Santa's eyes and an almost-halo around him, like a headshot of an old Hollywood movie star. He's a little too phony for my taste. A little slick.

I put the manual copy in the envelope and seal it, but I leave out the Santa picture page. I have no idea why someone would be copying this, but whoever it was must have left it on the machine and I didn't notice when I put the manual originals in the tray.

I flip the photo over. A press release is glued to the back. *Brady McCaffery*, it says. *The Celebrity Santa.*

> *One of the world's most popular and beloved*
> *Santas, Brady McCaffery has been touring*
> *the world, starring in films, television*
> *programs, commercials, and live events*
> *for more than twenty years. A sought-after*
> *guest at America's hottest celebrity parties,*

Santa Brady has headlined the holiday season for such notables as Amy Poehler, Usher, and soap opera star Montreat Cole. A top-rated motivational speaker, Santa Brady has held audiences of five hundred plus spellbound with his inspirational stories of the Magic of Christmas and the Power of Personality.

In the last few years, Santa Brady has shared his exceptional skills and experience with a select group of Santas-in-Training. This year, due to popular demand, he's expanding his Santa training schedule with exclusive, two-day seminars in five American cities. For more information about events in Orlando, Branson, Dallas, Las Vegas, and, of course, Hollywood, visit celebritysanta.net.

A list of some of Santa Brady's clients follows. Sony Pictures. Friends of the Los Angeles Zoo. Reese Witherspoon. Hallmark. Maybe that's why he's familiar? I saw him on a TV special?

Wait. There it is: *O, The Oprah Magazine.*

Aunt Carole had lived in faraway Los Angeles for most of my life. I'd seen her on a few of the not-too-busy-at-the-shop holidays. Fourth of July. Easter. She never visited at Christmas, but one time she came in October when Santa School was in session. I was probably eight or nine and I barely knew her, but suddenly there she was at the North Pole telling me I should go back home and get out of Grampa Chris's way when he had work to do. Thankfully, Grampa Chris showed up right then and told her not to fuss, that I was his special helper and that I should head on into Snowflake as I usually did. If he invited her to join too, I don't know, but she left the next day anyhow, and I don't remember seeing her again until after Grampa Chris died.

When she moved back to Hollydale, she pretty much

ignored me until one day, just a few weeks after my birthday, she came smiling into our kitchen saying she had a surprise for me. She was taking me on an adventure, one just perfect for a young girl of thirteen. I should be ready on Friday morning at ten, she said, and she would pick me up.

She did pick me up, but apparently I was not ready. Aunt Carole made me change out of my jeans and T-shirt and into a Peter Pan–collared dress she thought more suitable. And then she made me brush my hair. And then, after another look, made me tame my hair into a ponytail, the placement of which made it impossible to rest my head against the seatback for the whole of our two-and-a-half-hour drive. Aunt Carole herself was perfectly polished. She has the same pale skin as I do, but her hair is silver-white and cut in a severely angled bob. On that day, she was in head-to-toe black and she had on what I would soon learn were her signature sunglasses. A stack of bangles rattled on her wrist.

"*We* are going to a very special place," she said in the sort of slow singsong voice that people use with kindergarteners. "*We* will be making a good impression. This will include taking small bites, chewing with our mouths closed, and making quiet conversation."

"*I* can do that," I said, and I waited for her to say that she could, too, but she didn't. In fact, she didn't say much of anything until, two and a half hours later, we were in Chicago. I'd only been in the city once before, on a school field trip to the Shedd Aquarium. I loved the energy of the place, the people walking everywhere with shopping bags and fancy coats and looking like they have important places to be. I stared out the car window at the tall buildings and the elegant shops, marveling how different life could be just a few hours away from Hollydale.

Aunt Carole's car stopped at a light in front of a row of shops. A huge American Girl store dominated the corner, there were some standard-issue coffee shops and a shipping place, and what looked like a Macy's. There was also a very posh-looking restaurant across the street. Maybe she was taking me there for lunch?

Aunt Carole whipped around the corner and pulled into a nearby parking garage. "I should have asked if you had a dolly already, but don't worry, I'll buy you a new one if we need it," she said, angling the car into a spot.

Did she say *dolly*?

A minute later, we were standing in the middle of the American Girl store. It was sparkly and pink and filled with dolls that looked like perfect little girls and perfect little girls that looked like dolls. I would have loved it when I was seven or eight. But thirteen? Aunt Carole scanned the room, found a lady in an American Girl shirt, and strode toward her.

Was I supposed to follow?

I reached Aunt Carole just as she was asking the cornered employee about a Girl Scout troop meeting being held in a private room.

The lady looked skeptical. "Do you have an invitation?" she asked.

Aunt Carole jangled her jewelry. "I'm meeting someone."

The American Girl lady spoke with the practiced calm our Ms. Santas use on overzealous Instagram moms. "Ma'am," she said, her voice low. "I don't know what you've heard, but she's not here. She's just the sponsor. It's really a shoot for the magazine—"

"I don't want to meet *Oprah*," huffed Aunt Carole. Several nearby moms snapped to attention.

The saleslady noticed me then and shook her head. "I can't add her, ma'am. It's a private party."

Aunt Carole laughed, as if the idea of adding me to whatever it was they were talking about was completely ridiculous. "I just want to peek in and see my friend in action. You understand."

The lady looked at me again. Aunt Carole did too.

"Go over there." Aunt Carole pointed me toward a line of girls and moms and dolls waiting to get into the American Girl Cafe. "Tell them we have a one o'clock reservation. I'll join you in a minute."

I was seated at a small table in the corner and given a pretty pink menu. All around were tables of girls and moms and dolls, all age-appropriate and happy to be there. After a while, a server came over and refilled my glass of water. MARVEL, it said on his badge. "Are you waiting for someone?"

"My aunt," I said. "She said she'd be right back."

"You've been sitting here for fifteen minutes." He sounded suspicious, as if I had made up a fictitious aunt just so I could watch other girls feed their dolls while I drank all his water. "How about I bring you a Chocolate Chunky Marshmallow Square? A lot of moms won't let their kid have one once they know how gooey they are. Doll clothes stain," he said. "But you don't have a doll here."

"Or a mom," I said. I meant here with me, but Marvel reacted as if I had just told him I was an orphan.

"I'll warm it up for you," he said, patting my shoulder. "Be right back, honey."

Unlike Aunt Carole, Marvel kept his word. A moment later he was back and setting before me a pale pink plate on which sat a brick-size chocolate chunk brownie. Raspberry marshmallow sauce puddled at the sides. "What's your aunt's name, kiddo?" he asked.

I swallowed some brownie. "Carole."

Marvel nodded. "Well, you enjoy that. I'll be back to check on you in a bit."

Here is what you need to know about the Chocolate Chunky Marshmallow Square: Chocolate chunks, melty. Brownie cake, fudgy. Mini Marshmallows, baked inside and gooey. Raspberry marshmallow sauce, sticky.

Somewhere around bite six, I heard the telltale rattle of bracelets. It's remarkable how in a building filled with squealing kids and chattering parents, the rattle of silver bangles cuts through like a train whistle or a teacher barking your name in gym class.

Aunt Carole marched toward me, flanked by two American Girl employees. "She's *thirteen years old,*" she said, and unlike when she was proposing I get a dolly, thirteen now sounded old enough to warrant the purchase of life insurance. The look on her face suggested that might not be such a bad idea.

"She was fine; weren't you, Frankincense?" Her voice wavered as she reached the table. I seemed to have a little chocolate on my cheeks. Maybe on my sweater, too. And my pants.

"It is store policy—" began the manager, but she was interrupted by cheers from the surrounding tables. *Was* Oprah here?

"HO HO HO!"

I looked up, and even though I knew Grampa Chris had died, even though I had been in the Tree Shed and I went to the funeral and had heard over and over how Aunt Carole had moved back to Hollydale from California to help out with running the shop now that Grampa Chris was gone, even though I one hundred percent *knew* all those things, when I looked up, I believed I would see him. But of course I didn't.

The Santa I did see was a real-bearded Santa, like Grampa Chris had been, but at first I wasn't sure. There was a sheen to his beard that made me think maybe it was a yak hairpiece like the one Dad uses, but after another look it was clear he had just combed some glitter conditioner through it. He was wearing makeup, too. Not a lot. Just some mascara, it looked like, and some blush to make his cheeks rosy. His eyebrows had been whitened. It wasn't so much that any other kid would notice, but I am Christopher Wood's granddaughter. I know what it takes to make a Santa.

A table of five- and-six-year-olds cheered. "It's Santa!" they squealed. They couldn't believe their luck. Santa was here. In August! At the American Girl Cafe!

"Merry Christmas! Merry Christmas, everyone!" boomed this glittery Santa.

"I didn't see this on the schedule," said one of the American Girl ladies. The other one shrugged. "He was only supposed to be here for a private party. That one for Oprah's Girl Scout troop." She didn't actually *say* Oprah. She just mouthed it.

Aunt Carole raised her arm to wave at Santa and he nodded back at her and suddenly I became important. "Wipe your face!" she hissed. She dunked a napkin in my water glass and smooshed it on my cheek. "I leave you alone for five minutes," she muttered, as Santa began making his way from table to table. His reds, I noticed, were bright, his whites spotless, and his boots shone. His voice was deep, like Darth Vader's, and at every table I heard him tell girls they looked beautiful and he hoped they were being good. He laughed a lot and even though he wasn't saying anything funny, people laughed along with him like they were all following a script.

"And your hair," huffed Aunt Carole. She pinched one of the stray bits that was always falling out of my ponytail. It was pink and marshmallowy, and when Aunt Carole unpinched, my hair was still stuck to her finger. She yanked her hand away. Some of my hair went with it.

Which is when this Santa turned toward us. "Ho ho ho," he said.

"Hello, Santa," said Aunt Carole, her voice sweet as marshmallow sauce. "This is the young lady I was telling you about. My darling little niece, Francie."

"Of course I recognize Francine," said Santa, which was his first real mistake. Grampa Chris never used the name of a kid he didn't know. The possibility of messing it up—mishearing, mispronouncing, just plain forgetting—nothing will destroy the Santa Knows Everything myth quicker than screwing up a kid's name. It was clear to me that despite being so slick-looking, this guy could use a stint at Santa School.

"Is this real fur?" Aunt Carole put her hand on the Santa's arm. "It's luxurious. Just wonderful." Grampa Chris's Santa coat was wool. The cuffs were not real fur, but they were so soft he used to say they were spun from clouds.

"I've never seen someone work a room like this, Brady," said Aunt Carole.

"I have," I said.

"Eat your brownie, Francie." Aunt Carole turned her

back to me then, but I could still hear her cooing at Santa Slick. "Really, Brady, you're astonishing. I don't know how you do it."

A third American Girl lady appeared at our table to tell us that Santa's sleigh had arrived and it was time for him to go. Then when this fancy, phony Santa pulled a business card from his pocket. "I'm intrigued," he said to Aunt Carole. "Let's keep in touch." Aunt Carole reached for it, which was when she noticed the strands of my marshmallowed hair still stuck to her fingers. She pulled back in horror, sending the card flying. It landed on my plate, in the puddle of raspberry marshmallow glaze, the image of that slick, glittery Santa staring up at me out of the goo.

8

Another part of Hollydale High School's commitment to "authentic writing" is to make us pretend we're real writers with real writing groups. The idea is that we'll talk out our subjects and share our drafts and form lifelong bonds over discussions of symbolism and parallel sentence construction. In reality, it usually means that you talk about whatever you might talk about at lunch and occasionally correct each other's spelling.

Before Ms. Colando (*Totoro* shirt under fuzzy blue cardigan) finishes telling us that we'll be forming groups, I've made eye contact with DeKieser, who has done the same with Ellie Baptiste, junior, film geek. The theater kids are all together and the comic kids are all together too. As are Sam, Gunther, and the other puckheads, of course, but since there are six of them, Ms. Colando suggests they break up and join other groups. She nods at Gunther and I feel a chill run up my spine.

Thankfully, Ellie speaks before Gunther can get himself out of his chair. "We'll take Hector," she says, pulling a desk between the two of us and patting it. "Have you listened to him talk?" she whispers to DeKieser. "Prime voice-over material." Ellie has to make a short film for her Video Arts class, and even though she doesn't know what it will be about, she's already scouting locations and talent. "Hey, Hector," she says, aiming her phone camera. "Say 'In a world where testosterone rules, one man leaves the safety of his clan to join three smart women in an against-all-odds struggle to stay awake during first-period English.'"

"I'm not doing your movie, E," Hector says. He does have a really great voice. Sort of rumbly. He slides into the seat beside me and another shiver rolls up my spine, but for very different reasons.

"We'll see." Ellie drops her phone in her pocket before Ms. Colando spies it. Phones are not allowed in classrooms, but of course everyone has one.

Ms. Colando continues. "You'll spend the last fifteen minutes of class sharing with each other one topic you intend to explore this quarter and what leads you to believe that topic has a mythology worth spending time on. I don't expect you to have figured out what you want to say about the topic—in fact, if you already know what you want to say, pick something else. This quarter is about exploration, not about confirming what you already know."

"Better not write about what it is to be a stud, then," Gunther says, slapping Sam on the shoulder.

Hector looks down at his desk and I get the feeling that he is as grateful to Ellie for calling him away from the puckheads as I am, which, of course, makes me think of Alice's stupid PDA plan. Just like that, stomach flips, neck prickles, and the slow burn of a crimson blush threatens my cheeks. Thankfully Ms. Colando starts talking again.

For the next sixty minutes of our seventy-five minute Mythology Today class she tells us about a couple of French scholars who would have agreed with all the definitions we came up with on Tuesday, but who mostly argued that myth is a "system of meaning" and that you could break stories apart and look at underlying oppositions like brave/cowardly, pure/tainted, right/wrong and tell what sort of culture the stories supported. The tricky bit was that different myths contradicted one another and sometimes a myth contradicted itself, and this, she said, was what made studying myth "fun."

"Your explorations may require research—some historical, some contemporary—and a great deal of thought. While you may choose a different topic each week, I believe that by digging deeply into elements of a single topic—say, golf or pet stores or Marvel characters—you will have a richer experience."

Ellie, it appears, has been thinking a lot about this

already. "So," she says, "I'm going to do the mythology of teen film comedies, like how they define teenagers and how they should behave and what values they should hold." Ellie has dark, sproingy hair and wears glasses with big bold frames which, according to DeKieser, she doesn't really need for seeing but make her feel more "directorial," like Spike Lee or Ava DuVernay. I understand this choice. When I first came to Hollydale as a freshman, I wore my mom's Dr. Martens all the time. I don't think anyone else thought they were particularly cool, but they were so heavy they made me feel a little tougher during those first few weeks when my doubts about choosing Hollydale over Regina were greatest.

Ellie spends about thirteen minutes telling us which films she's going to watch and who is in the films and who the directors are and which ones suck. Then she turns it over to DeKieser, who says she isn't sure what she's going to do yet. Or what the oppositions are. Or whatever.

"You're not going to do hockey, are you?" Ellie asks Hector.

"There's more to life than hockey," rumbles Hector. I shiver again, then look around as if searching for a draft. Oh, holy night.

Ms. Colando taps her pen on her lectern and reminds us that we only have a few minutes left. "I've heard some people say they don't have any ideas about what to explore. Perhaps it would be helpful to think about something you don't understand, but want to—" Somebody from Sam's group mumbles and there is more laughter.

It would be ridiculous to think the puckheads are talking about me, but I feel my cheeks vermillionize, anyway. If Alice were here she'd raise a supportive eyebrow at me, but as far as I know, DeKieser and Ellie have no knowledge of my first-kiss humiliation. Hector might, but he's keeping his eyes on his notebook, so I can't tell for sure.

Ms. Colando makes her patiently-waiting-for-an-elevator face, then continues. "Things that annoy you can be good starting places too."

"Maybe hockey *teammates* are a possibility," Hector says, and the rest of us laugh. "At least I wouldn't have to do much research. Hockey eats up a lot of homework time."

Hector is not only rumble-voiced and funny, he is smart. I may not play a sport but my shifts at the shop are going to increase as the season rolls on, and if I'm really going to Pillar Point my way to a Miata, I'm not going to be able to complain about hours or beg off for homework. Choosing something that would be easy to research is a good idea.

"I'm doing Christmas," I say.

"We aren't allowed to, like, do, you know, religion and stuff."

"Secular Christmas," I clarify. "Santa. Trees. Holly."

"Elves," adds Ellie.

"Yes," I say, remembering what Ms. Colando said about things that annoy. "I'll start with elves."

9

NOVEMBER 6

On Sundays my family goes to Mass in shifts so that, as my dad says, "some of us can be working at the shop while the others are praying for it." This morning Uncle Jack is working with Dad on a Santa's Village display, and Mom is here with Dash, Don, Gram, and me, which means we'll get out of here quicker than we do when Uncle Jack is around. Uncle Jack is popular with the widows of the church, and no recessional hymn is complete without at least one of them putting a hand on his arm and inviting him over for supper or out to a movie. With Mom, we're out the door before Father Tim has made it down the aisle.

I was supposed to hang out with Alice after Mass, but she texted me this morning to say she had to cover a basketball game at Saint Lawrence because the sports beat person was sick. **Carly and Margo and a couple other Regina girls will be there. Want to come?** I was friends with Carly and Margo when we all went to Our Lady of Sorrows, but when I see them now it feels awkward, like catching a show you used to watch when you were little. There's some temporary nostalgia value, but after a few minutes you find yourself kind of detached and wondering how you ever really believed that noseless Arthur was actually an aardvark. If I went to the game, Alice would be doing her reporter thing and I'd be stuck with people I barely know anymore until somebody's parent was able to take me home.

If I'd have gone to Regina, like Alice did, would I feel the same way? Or would I be almost as close to Carly and the others as I am to Alice? Probably not. Alice has been my best friend since she moved to Hollydale from Michigan in fifth grade. On the first day of school she arrived without a lunch and wearing our school uniform, unaware that Our Lady of Sorrows didn't require uniforms during the inaugural two days of school, nor would Hilda DeSmet, head cook, provide hot lunch until Monday.

Alice is a little shorter than I am now, but back then she was positively minuscule and looked so small and lonely in the cafeteria without friends or a lunch or anything. I gave her half of my tomato-and-cheese sandwich and a homemade brownie for which, I told her, my grandmother was famous. The next day, I wore my uniform even though I didn't have to (the first and only time I would wear a uniform by choice, I should note) and Alice brought her own lunch, which included a small Tupper-ware container of kimchi that she said her grandmother had made and for which she was famous too.

I'll be honest. It took me a few months before I started liking kimchi, but I liked Alice right away, so I ate what she gave me and said thank you and she said you're wel-come and just like that we were friends, and nothing as stupid as going to different schools is going to stop us from being friends either. That said, I'll feel better when I've earned enough to Miata my way to and from basketball games by myself.

I texted Alice that it was okay and I'd see her after school tomorrow. I've got a Mythology Today explora-tion to do anyway. Also, I found a note from Bryan in my in-box reminding me to fill out my uniform evaluation form and return it and the uniform itself to Aunt Carole's office ASAP.

When we get home from Mass, I find the form and fill it in.

UNIFORM EVALUATION:
Breathability: Poor. Sometimes caught my reflection in countertops and windows, which made breathing difficult for several minutes afterward.
Cleanability: Outfit prompted looks from customers, which made me feel unclean.
Durability: Too durable. Repeated attempts to set fire to vest proved unsuccessful.

Visibility: See "Restriction of Movement."

Restriction of Movement: Severe shame associated with being seen in uniform restricted me to stockroom/backroom.

Comments: Never before have I been so grateful to end a week of work—and I've manned the face painting booth during the Easter Bunny Bonanza, so that's saying something.

Aunt Carole doesn't come to the office most Sundays, so I drop my evaluation sheet and uniform on her desk and then I head to Snowflake to do a little elf research. There are some transcripts of Grampa Chris's old *An Evening with Santa* shows on the table, proof that my dad has been in here practicing. Like I said before, he's a pretty natural Santa in most ways, but going on television isn't easy for him.

I stack the transcripts in a pile and flip through the Santa School manual for some of Grampa Chris's elf material. The good thing about Ms. Colando's exploration papers is that she doesn't care if they are formal or organized. We're just supposed to do some researching and thinking and then dash off a one-to-two-page response, which should be pretty easy, especially for this topic. I've been thinking about elves—or how to avoid them—for most of my life.

The thing is, in popular culture the people who take jobs as Santa's elves are usually portrayed as burned out, desperate, no-other-options-available-and-I-have-to-pay-the-bills types. My experience with elves is different. People who apply for elf training at Santa School are energetic, enthusiastic, and eager. They list "ability to turn cartwheels" among their marketable skills. They won't let you call them Derek or BethAnne but insist on being referred to by their elf identity. Spangles, for example. Or Flip. They juggle. They use squeaky voices. They enjoy noisy clothes. Bells are common. Kazoo necklaces and bicycle horn noses are not unheard of. They are loud, grinning, exhausting people who have no real knowledge of or care for their own origin story or place in Christmas lore.

In the manual, Grampa Chris explains that the notion of the elf as Santa's workforce showed up for the first time in 1873 in *Godey's Lady's Book*, which was, essentially, the *Cosmopolitan* of the nineteenth century, if *Cosmo* didn't have *Glamour* and *Elle* and *Vogue* and the internet for competition. Basically, *Godey's Lady's Book* was it for women's media, and as soon as they dropped a couple of hammer-toting elves on the front cover, the story was legit. Elves made toys for Santa. The end.

The *Godey's* elves didn't dance. They didn't frolic. There was not a kazoo in sight. We can assume, from the illustration, that they were content in their employment. But giddy? Forget it. They were dedicated, responsible workers. Not scene-stealing showboats.

What changed?

Commercialism, probably. The thing is, the bigger the

Santa story grew, the more merchandising opportunities came with it. And with merchandising and marketing came more and more people wanting a piece of the Christmas pie. But no matter how big the Christmas Industrial Complex grows, there's only one star of the Christmas show, of course. Santa.

Actually, my Grampa Chris would say the star of the show is the child. Each child. One child at a time. That Santa's sole purpose is to make that child feel seen and valued and cared for and loved. Which is the opposite of showboat elvery.

I write all that down and then identify a few oppositions I can mention in class, including self-centered/ child-centered, behind-the-scenes/on stage, and real/fake. The last one isn't exactly right, I know. I mean, even the quiet, hardworking elves of *Godey's* aren't exactly *real*. But they aren't fake either.

10

Monday morning. Six a.m. Somehow, between the time that I fell asleep last night and the time that Santa-in-the-Chimney *ho*ed his first morning *ho*, a Texas Christmas Monstrosity has appeared in my bedroom closet.

Details: Cranberry dress with yoke shoulders and silver snap closures. Silver belt. Silver snakeskin cowboy boots. A tin star is affixed to left breast pocket. SHERIFF OF SNOWTOWN, it says. A note is pinned to the sleeve.

> *F:*
>
>   *Carole read your last evaluation and asked me to clarify the definitions of the survey words for you. By breathability, we mean: Does the uniform make you sweat? By*

visibility, we mean: Does the uniform make
it easy for customers to find you and identify
you as a Hollydale Holiday Shop team
member? As for durability, it is unnecessary
to put the uniform to test conditions beyond
those that would be encountered in a normal
workday. We hope that these clarifications
will help you in your evaluative processes
and provide us with the sort of useful data
we desire. Enjoy this week's uniform. We
look forward to seeing your response.
That's the holiday spirit!
Bryan

PS: The hat is on your dresser.

I turn around. There is a hat on my dresser. A carmine
cowboy hat with silver holly leaf band.

PPS: Because of the difficulty of obtaining
customer evaluations when you are in the
stockroom, you have been assigned to the
salesfloor beginning tomorrow. Enjoy!

At school, I see the tongues of two varsity puckheads and
two freshmen I don't even know.

"It's spreading," I tell Alice after school.

"You need to seriously consider PDA," Alice reiterates.

I don't tell her that I have been considering it—or at least that my dreams have been. For the last two nights, I've had driving-around-town Miata dreams again, but in one of them it isn't Michael B. along for the ride, but various members of the Hollydale student body. At least, I think it is various members. The only one I can actually remember gazing back at me from the passenger seat is Hector Ramirez. "No," I tell her again.

"Then you're going to have to talk to Sam in private. Explain that his secret is safe with you."

"Aren't you supposed to say 'Just ignore it'? 'If you don't give the boys the attention they want, they'll stop'?"

"Sure," she says. "Or I could tell you to ask Santa Claus for help."

We're in Snowflake. Santa Franklin has called Dad again, asking if we have any photos of him from the years he was a student. He's come to Santa School five times, so I've got five photo albums to look through. We do Santa School old school. We actually print out photos and make albums. Which reminds me, making this year's album is on my list of nonstore jobs to do. I'm not even assigned to do it, really. I took it on thinking I could get a few points in the Initiative Pillar. Except it has already been six weeks since Santa School ended and I've been so busy working at the shop and "experiencing" uniforms and blushing over dream boys who wouldn't even notice me in real life that I haven't printed a single image. I need to get on that.

"Is that him?" asks Alice. She's pointing to one of a dozen Santas in a group photo. They're all in full-on regalia, so it is kind of hard to tell. Thankfully two of the Santas are Black (which Santa Franklin isn't) and one is tall and skinny (ditto), so that rules out three from the start.

"Write down 'forty-seven.' We'll make him a copy just in case."

Alice and I flip through some more pages, marking down the numbers on the photos. We've got them backed up on the computer and normally we would just email him a connection to the file, but the flood destroyed his computer too. And his electricity. Basically his house is kind of ruined. Where he's going to put a bunch of Santa photos in a ruined house I have no idea. But he asked Dad and Dad asked me and I can use a Pillar Point and so there it is.

We're just opening the last album when we hear someone in the next classroom over. A lot of times people from the various ornament and decor manufacturers come to meet with Dad or Mom or one of the other buyers and they spread their samples out on the tables in there.

"We're barely breaking even, Nick." It's Aunt Carole and, by the sound of it, Dad. I put my finger to my lips so Alice won't say anything. I wouldn't mind Aunt Carole seeing that I'm doing this work for Santa Franklin, but she has this thing about me having friends in the shop or the North Pole. No friends in the workplace, she says, which is easy for her to say, since as far as I can tell she doesn't have friends anyplace.

"All we need to do is break even, Carole. The school is more of a service than a business."

You tell her, Dad.

"That attitude was fine when Dad was alive. It was his passion, his little charity project, bringing together Santas and elves and all the other holiday oddballs he could find. But Dad is gone, Nick. And you don't even like doing it."

"I like doing it," I hear my dad say, though I have to admit, he isn't entirely convincing.

"You hate it," says Aunt Carole, her bangles clanking for emphasis. "You hate the cable show, for sure."

"*Dad* loved it," my father says. "And I love these people who loved Dad. I'm not closing the school, Carole." I can't see him, him being in the front parlor classroom and me here in Snowflake, but I know the look on his face. He has his head tilted down so he can look up over the frame of his glasses. His brow is furrowed, his mouth serious. It's a look that shuts down pushy salespeople, bad employees, and, on occasion, his misbehaving children. It's a look that says *enough*.

Apparently Aunt Carole can't read the look. Or she's not looking at him. She persists, though I notice that her voice has gotten softer. So soft that I make Alice stop flipping scrapbook pages so I can hear. "That is the point, Nicholas. You don't have to close the school. We can keep Dad's dream alive. It's more of a partnership than anything. And with Brady, we'll get even more publicity and many more students. We'll have to do half as much work and we'll make twice as much money. Maybe more."

"Hollywood Santa," says Dad. He sounds disgusted. *I'm* disgusted. Is she really suggesting that we hand Grampa Chris's school over to Santa Slick?

"I've seen him in action, Nicholas. He's very good. If you'd just watch the videos I sent you."

"I don't have time for videos," he says. "I don't have time for any of this." *Tell her, Dad. Tell her she can't kill Grampa Chris's school.*

"But you would if you had help." Aunt Carole again. "Brady is offering us a franchise. We can be part of his tour. Nicholas—" I can feel a fire-red rage building in my gut and I'm about to bust in there and tell her she can go back to Hollywood herself if she thinks it's so great, but Alice stops me before I get halfway to the door.

"Miata," she whispers. Alice wants me to buy Uncle Jack's car as much as I do.

"As long as the school is breaking even, Carole, we're keeping it in-house. If someday things change, we'll talk about it."

"It might be too late then," says Aunt Carole. "He'll find another venue. Another partner . . ." I'm guessing she sees Dad's face now, because she pauses. "So . . . as long as the school keeps breaking even . . ."

Dad must lose all patience with the conversation because he ends it. "I'm needed in Nativity," he says.

Alice and I hear Dad leave, and then Aunt Carole leaves too, her bracelets rattling into the distance.

Alice shakes her head. "She does not take no for an answer, does she?"

"She is *not* going to get rid of the Santa School," I say.

Alice's face turns as giddy as it does for molasses cookies and her Miss Fisher voice kicks in strong. "Are you saying you have a plan?"

"I don't need a plan. You heard my dad. The Santa School just needs to keep breaking even. It doesn't need to make more money, or expand, or anything else. All I have to do is help my dad keep everything exactly as it is."

"No plan?" Alice sounds genuinely disappointed.

"You don't need a plan," I tell her, "if you don't want anything to change."

11

For an entire week I wear my Holiday Hoedown gear at the shop. It is worse than the Nightmare on Elf Street uniform. The hat limits my vision so I'm always bumping into and tripping over things—displays, customers, and, most tragically, a five-foot-tall inflatable Frosty ($67.50) who proves no match for the pointy tin star on my chest. The boots are the worst part. By the end of the week I have four blisters and am hobbling around like the Winter Warlock before he learns to put one foot in front of the other.

The number of tongue sightings at school stays relatively stable, though, and nobody bothers me during Ms. Colando's class, which is a relief. My exploration sharing goes well too. By the time it's my turn to share with my group, I've thought a little more about the mythology involved and am able to tell them how the original work-shop elf served the purpose of erasing the economics of the holiday.

"It covered over consumerism by suggesting that all the toys were made at the North Pole," I explain. "The addition of elves to the mythology of Christmas helped hide the reality of the dollars that had to change hands in order for presents to appear under the family tree."

DeKieser is appalled. "Whoa," she says. "That, like, sucks."

I admit that it does. Then I tell her how that particular mythology persists, but the elves themselves—at least the ones who apply to Santa School—have added ego to the mix. How they've become showy and attention seeking.

"Elves used to be background players," I say. "They used to be more modest. More . . ." I search for the right word.

Hector comes to my rescue. "Elf-effacing?" he suggests.

I can't help but laugh. Ellie can't either, nor can she help but add on.

"Now they're smug and elf-satisfied," she says. "No elf-respect. No elf-discipline. Always posing for elfies." She adjusts her glasses and holds up her phone like she's going to snap a shot.

Ms. Colando gives us her waiting-for-an-elevator look. "Perhaps you should move on to the next exploration?" she says. "DeKieser, have you presented yet?"

DeKieser digs around in her backpack for some of the

college brochures that have flooded her family's mailbox, and as she does, Hector touches my arm. Instant goose bumps.

Oh, holy night.

He leans toward me, his face growing close to mine, and even though I *know-know-know* it's only so he can tell me something, a weak-kneed part of my brain associates the gesture with every rom-com movie kiss it has ever witnessed. Just like that—capillaries fire, stomach flips, neck prickles. Hector's lips pause just a few inches away from my ear.

"I hope you don't feel like I was making fun of *you* or anything." He says it quietly enough that nobody else around will hear. He's not being performative or jokey. It's genuine kindness, but, I tell myself, it is *not* a kiss. Not even close. "I hope I didn't go too far," he says.

You didn't go far enough, says the weak-kneed part of my brain.

As if you'd know what to do if he did, says the rest.

"I'm fine," I say to Hector. "I mean, um, it's always open season on the elves, as far as I'm concerned."

DeKieser finally locates the brochures she was looking for and drops them on her desk, but it turns out she has something else on her mind. "So, um, I was thinking about the, like, oppositions and whatever," she says. "Like, what if you think both parts of the opposition are true, like, you think that an elf is both selfish and giving?"

The discussion of elves pulls me back from my weakkneedness just enough for a calming bit of snark. "Impossible," I tell her.

"I don't know," says Hector, who has returned to his less-blushingly-close seated position. "F. Scott Fitzgerald thought that the ability to hold two opposed ideas at the same time was the sign of a first-rate intelligence."

Ellie snorts derisively. "In Psych that's called cognitive dissonance—it's one of the great stressors of modern life."

Hector turns to me as if I will be the tiebreaker in this argument. My stomach flips again and even though I should be seriously considering intelligence and stress, I find myself thinking about Alice's PDA plan, knowing it would likely work for anyone else, but for me is doomed before it even begins. "Maybe," I say, "it's both."

12

UNIFORM EVALUATION #2:

Cowboy Christmas

Breathability: None.

Cleanability: Wipeable, like a plastic tablecloth.

Durability: Snakeskin boots lost a lot of silver, appeared to be shedding.

Visibility: Practically reflective.

Restriction of Movement: Belt not made for cookie lovers. More important, the boots gave me blisters.

Comments: Kill me now, pardner.

COMMENTS FROM CUSTOMER EVALUATIONS:

The girl was cute but her uniform made me think I would find more Western-themed ornaments and

I only found five, one of which was a pink Stetson and I wanted blue for my nephew.

The boots are darling! Sparkly! I would wear them if I could get away with it.

Employee could have smiled more. She almost looked embarrassed to be there.

13

Uniform three: White button-down shirt. Candy cane-striped tie and knee socks. Cranberry suspenders. Pin-striped shorts. "Appropriate shoes of your choosing."

I'm still battling my cowboy-boot blisters so I put on my old Dr. Martens, which are the roomiest footwear I own. The worst part of the uniform is the suspenders. I can't decide if they are supposed to ride over the crest of the boobs or outside them? Or should I forget my shoulders entirely and let the suspenders dangle from my waistband? I try a different option each day of my "Corporate Christmas" week. On Friday, I put them on backward, so the crisscross part is in the front, which may not be the most appropriate option, but surprisingly is the most comfortable.

Dottie, the floor supervisor for the day, stations me at the inside entrance to the shop, in front of a table full of turkey platters. She pulls a folded-up piece of paper from her apron pocket and reads it.

"You're supposed to smile and say, 'Welcome to the Hollydale Holiday Shop' to each guest." She says it with an enthusiasm one usually reserves for closet cleaning and dental appointments. I like Dottie.

"Each guest? What if they are in a group?" I ask.

Dottie raises one shoulder, not even committed enough to the prospect to give me a full shrug. "You're the one who pissed Carole off. You figure it out."

"I didn't piss her off," I say. "She's just evil."

Dottie shrugs the other shoulder. "Offer maps to everyone, but the tour bus people get full welcome packets." She hands me a Crayola-red bucket ($4.95) filled with brochures and maps and discount coupons.

"Are there are lot of buses scheduled today?"

Dottie grunts and puts the instruction sheet in my free hand. "Weekend before Thanksgiving? We've got four booked for this afternoon. Never know when the rogues will come in. Let me know when you need more brochures."

I can see a couple of ladies I recognize from the library heading in from the parking lot. Dottie sees them too. She turns to face me, showing her back to the door. "Just a heads-up," she says quietly. "Your aunt's intern has one of those cameras aimed right at this spot."

She's right. There are two security cameras above the front doors. One is pointed at the registers, as it usually is, but the other is aimed squarely at me. It is possible that Bryan is watching my performance right now. I salute the camera. Sleigh bells ring as the front door opens. "You're on, kiddo," says Dottie. "Smile for the people."

"Welcome to the Hollydale Holiday Shop," I say, which startles Mrs. Fenderson, the library's Storytime Lady.

"Hello, Francie," she says when she's recovered. "Aren't you something?"

"I am," I say. "Would you like a map?"

"I've been here a hundred times, Francie. I don't need a map any more than you do."

I try not to look at the camera. "Just following orders, ma'am."

Mrs. Fenderson winces sympathetically. "Hard to believe it is already *An Evening with Santa* day," she says. "This season is just flying by."

Try standing here in elfin business attire all afternoon, I want to tell her. *That'll stop time in its tracks.*

Mrs. Fenderson and her friend head for Paper Goods and I am left alone with the brochure bucket and the sounds of the Andrews Sisters *Ja-ja-ja-jingl*ing all the way. Their harmonies are temporarily interrupted by Dottie, who is using the PA system to call my dad to the Tree Shed. I try not to picture him there. Instead, I focus on what a surprise it is that he is working on *An Evening with Santa* day. Grampa Chris never did. He considered it one of the most important days of the season and made sure he was dressed and rested and across the street at the library's public access cable studio long before it was time for the live broadcast. Of course, he had Gram and Dad and Mom and Uncle Jack to run the shop while he was away. Now there's just Mom and Uncle Jack to cover while he's gone, and as wonderful as Uncle Jack is, he's not particularly managerial, so nobody feels right leaving him in charge of anything.

Plus, I suppose Dad isn't really in a hurry to get to the studio. *An Evening with Santa* isn't exactly his favorite part of the Santa gig. He's really good at all the in-person stuff—kids in a Santa line, waving from a parade float—but the on-camera stuff makes him nervous. Really nervous. I mean, he's good once things start, but beforehand he's a wreck, so for the past two years I've been going with him to keep him calm so he doesn't totally freak out and have a heart attack or . . . something . . . anyway, it's my job to go to the studio and prep him before the show. But first I need to put in some Miata-earning hours here at the shop.

There aren't a lot of customers at first, so I kill time straightening the platters, which seems like a Pillar kind of thing to do. Buses come in. I greet. I hand out brochures. Lunch is a welcome break, but then I'm back on the salesfloor, waiting for tourists. Most of the afternoon I find myself staring across the parking lot at the back of the North Pole, watching other employees come and go from their breaks. I am reminded that this building in which I am standing was once a dairy barn and imagine the cows who passed their days staring out these doors in much the same way. I tell myself I should make the most of the downtime by practicing verb conjugation for French class or planning future Mythology Today explorations, but as soon as I think of Mythology Today I am thinking of Hector Ramirez and the not-kiss. Okay, and more than once I imagine it as a not-not-kiss. I imagine he actually is leaning over to kiss me, that he wants to kiss me, right there in the middle of Mythology Today. The first time, I imagine the jaws of Sam Spinek and Gunther Hobbes dropping, but after that my daydreams turn purely Hector-centric. And very realistic. So realistic that I am glad the security camera isn't infrared, as I'm sure the rush of heat I feel each time would set off every alarm in the store. It is a very enjoyable way to pass the time.

I fan myself with Dottie's instruction sheet and notice a handwritten note from Bryan at the bottom. *Please remind Francine that she is on probation and that Carole is actively seeking an opportunity to discuss her employment with the management team.*

She means that Aunt Carole is going to talk to Dad about me and argue, yet again, that I'm not mature enough for this job. Lucky for me, Dad has been too busy at the shop to make time for such a discussion, but I know that I had better get in a few peak Pillar days before it happens. I glance at the cameras again as a Senior MidWest luxury tour bus pulls up in front of the entrance. Before any of the seniors can disembark, a little girl of about five or six pushes open the big front door and steps inside.

"Welcome to the Hollydale Holiday Shop!" I say with a Pillar-perfect grin.

"Are you an elf?" asks the girl.

"Heck no."

"What are you?"

I glance at the camera. "I'm Santa's Intern."

Sleigh bells ring and a crush of MidWest senior citizens push through the doors. "Welcome to the Hollydale Holiday Shop!" I say, and then I remember about the welcome brochures and start thrusting them into the hands of the seniors, who stop their forward motion to unfold them. There's getting to be a bit of a senior logjam.

I shout my welcomes a few more times before I feel a tug on my shirt.

"Feels like a cotton poly blend," the tugger says to the woman beside her.

"I knew it. The shorts look like a gabardine," she says. "Do you mind if I look at the tag, dear?" Her fingers are flipping the back of my waistband and she's cocking her head so she can read the label inside.

I stop myself from slapping her hand just in time. "What are you doing?" I say, remembering to smile. "I mean, can I help you?"

"There's no way to fill this in properly without knowing the fabric content," says the lady with the fingers. "You're right, Barbara. It's a wool gabardine."

"The shorts are made of wool," Barbara calls to the other seniors in the group. They have all fished pens out of their purses and are scribbling on one of the pages from the welcome packet.

"Are they constricting?" asks a tall lady near the pilgrim pyramid.

"Are they constricting?" Barbara asks me.

"They're okay, I guess. But why are you—"

Barbara flashes the page she's scribbling on. "There's a twenty percent off coupon for anyone who fills in this evaluation," she says, surveying the form again. "I think I'd give you a four for welcoming presence. The suspenders are a little off-putting."

"I'm not convinced about the constriction," says the tall lady. "Is she able to bend over?"

"Can you bend over?" asks the original tugger.

"Yeah, bend over," says another voice. A boy's voice.

The little girl has emerged from the swarm of tourists, led to safety by a dark-haired, dimple-cheeked boy in a Hollydale High School jacket. Sam Spinek.

Oh, holy night.

14

"**My brother needs** you to tell him *welcome*," says the girl.

Sam Spinek is just standing there among the throng of discount-seeking seniors, grinning at me. His dimple is double-deep and he looks very smug. "Welcome," I say in the least welcoming voice I can muster.

"Thank you," says Sam, "but I'm afraid I won't feel truly welcome until I know you're not constricted."

Barbara shoots him a disapproving look, then turns her attention back to me.

"I'm not constricted," I tell her. I flap my arms a couple of times for proof.

"I can't see the back," calls another lady.

"They need to see the back," says Sam.

"I'm not turning around," I say to him.

"Shut your eyes, Sammy," says the girl. "She doesn't want you to look at her butt."

I feel my face go crimson (rage, not modesty), but thankfully one of the tour ladies puts her map of the store over Sam Spinek's eyes. "Go ahead, sweetheart. Let us see the back and then we'll leave you be."

I turn around. The ladies scribble their assessments. When their bus driver reminds them that it is 5:45 and they only have a half hour left to shop, they thank me and move deeper into the store, eager to see what there is that they might want 20% off of.

"I'll take one of those evaluation forms," says Sam, reaching for my brochure bucket.

I yank the bucket away. "Get lost," I tell him.

"My sister needs a pilgrim hat for her school play," he says. "If I fill in a form, I get twenty percent off, right?"

"I'll give you twenty percent off if you *don't* fill it in," I say to Sam. "Aisle three," I tell his sister, who runs off in that direction. Sam, however, stays put.

"It must be hard to come to work like that," he says. "Are you sure you're not uncomfortable?"

"Less uncomfortable than I am at school with you and your goons harassing me." There. I said it. I only wish Alice were here to witness it.

"Harassing you?"

I stick out my tongue and then remember Bryan's watchful eye. I fake like it's part of a cough, covering my mouth for the camera.

"I don't do that," Sam says. "I've never done that."

"Your puckhead teammates do."

"Not all of them," he says.

It's true. Nobody bothers me in Mythology Today anymore, and Hector has never once stuck out his tongue at me, probably because he is a really nice guy, although maybe, it occurs to me, it's because he doesn't want me to think about him and kissing in the same moment.

"Besides, I can't control my friends," Sam continues.

"I think you can," I tell him.

Sam taps on a turkey platter. "Really," he says, stepping even closer, "I think this is in *your* control."

I'm careful not to laugh in a way that can be seen on camera. "Oh yeah? How's that?"

"You need to prove them wrong," he says. And then, just like Alice did, he tells me I should get a boyfriend and demonstrate my abilities in the school hallway.

I don't say anything.

And then Sam laughs. "Oh," he says. "Now I understand."

"You don't understand a thing," I say. But it turns out he does.

"How many guys have you kissed since me?" he asks. "Three? Two? Wait. I know. None?"

A green-haired lady with a stroller walks by. "Welcome to the Hollydale Holiday Shop," I say.

Sam moves closer. "I'm sorry about what happened," he says, almost like he means it. "I can't take back what I said to those guys, but I'm sorry. And I'd like to make it up to you."

"You would?" Okay. So maybe Alice was right. Maybe all I had to do was confront Sam Spinek and talk with him, person to person.

The doors of the Holiday Shop jingle open and three more women come in. "Welcome to the Hollydale Holiday Shop," I say.

Sam tugs at my sleeve, pulls me closer to him so he can talk quietly.

"When do you get off work?" he asks. "I could drop my sister off at home and come back for you. We could go make out."

"We could what?" Mrs. Fenderson has come back into view, and my desire not to make a spectacle of myself in front of the Storytime Lady is the only thing that keeps me from shouting.

"Make out. Like I said, I owe you."

My brain tsunamis with a million objections but the one that spills out is the dumbest. "You're going out with Ginger Smee."

Sam smiles generously. "I'm not going to *go* out with you. I'm going to *make* out with you. Give you a little practice. Then you'll be all ready for the next guy."

I need words. I have no words.

"If you want," he says, "I bet I can even find you a boy-friend for a party or two. That will prove everyone wrong and"—Sam snaps his fingers—"no more rude gestures."

I still have no words, so I respond with a single-digit

rude gesture of my own, one perfectly appropriate for the moment, if not for the setting.

"Frances!" gasps Mrs. Fenderson.

"I'm sorry. Oh, I didn't mean you. I'm—" Suddenly I have a lot of words, all apologetic, all doing little to decrease Sam's amusement or Mrs. Fenderson's horror. And then, out of the corner of my eye, I see the steady, alarm-red light of the store security camera and realize that they may not have been the only witnesses.

Oh, holy night.

"I'm sorry," I say again. "I . . . I have to go . . . on break. They're very strict here," I tell Mrs. Fenderson. I push a brochure into her hands. "There's a—there's a coupon on the form. Twenty percent off . . . I have to—"

Sam Spinek laughs as I dash out the front doors of the Holiday Shop and across the parking lot. There's a chance that Bryan wasn't watching just now. She might have just been recording me, thinking she'd watch at a more convenient time, like when she's plugged into an outlet charging her batteries. My only chance is to sneak into Aunt Carole's office and mess with the recording.

I race across the parking lot and into the North Pole. I take the stairs two at a time and have just cut through Accounting when I see her. "Brittany," I say. I study Bryan's face for any hint that she has seen me flip off a customer. Futile. She's as readable as a toaster.

"Francesca," she says. "I believe you have those suspenders on backward."

"Your beliefs are well-founded," I say, and then I wish I hadn't. I don't think I could ever count Bryan as an ally, but surely being snotty is not going to help my cause. I peek past her and into Aunt Carole's office. I can see the screen with the security images on it, but the office is dark.

"Is she here?" I ask. It would be worse if Aunt Carole had seen. Way worse.

"She went to the cable studio," she says. "For the show? She wanted to prep Santa."

I look at the clock. It's six o'clock. Stupid Sam Spinek made me lose track of time!

I'm the one who is supposed to prep Santa. If I know Carole, she's just making things worse, making him more anxious, more . . . I glance at the security monitor one more time. I'll have to take care of it later, after the show. First, I need to save Santa.

15

For the last thirty years our local cable access station, situated in the basement of the Hollydale Public Library, has hosted *An Evening with Santa.* For twenty-eight of those years, my Grampa Chris sat in the plush green Santa chair while a local TV personality introduced him and asked a few questions before turning to the call-in portion of the show. Kids from all over Hollydale would call in and ask questions and tell Santa what they wanted for Christmas. Obviously the show is carried live, although sometimes repeat broadcasts of the taped version are mixed in with the standard schedule of city council meetings and high school basketball games.

When Don and Dash were just babies, I would watch the show from Gram's house. I'd sit on her yellow sofa in my Dora the Explorer pajamas and Gram would turn on the television and the music would start. "Santa Claus Is Coming to Town," instrumental, heavy on the horns. A grainy image of a fireplace and stockings would appear on the screen, the words "An Evening with Santa" laid over it in fancy imperial-red script. "An Evening with Santa," Gram would say, as if reading the title of a book she was about to open. And then the fireplace image would disappear and the pomegranate face of cable access manager Pinky Donovan would come on and he would look straight into the camera and tell all the boys and girls of Hollydale that tonight was a special night. We would already know that, of course. We would already know that this was the special night when Santa Claus himself was in *our* town, in *our* local TV station, waiting to talk to *us*. Pinky Donovan would keep talking, telling us what a treat this was and how we could call the number on the screen, and even though I know now that his introduction lasts less than a minute, back then it felt like he would never stop talking and the camera would never show us what we most wanted to see. And then, when we thought we'd burst, there he would be. Santa Claus.

I must have known, even when I was very little, that the man on the TV was my Grampa Chris. I had seen him dressed as Santa dozens of times. I had seen his suit hanging in his bedroom closet and his boots polished and waiting by the door. He had a naturally white beard year-round and there was no mistaking his long thin nose for anyone

16

After a full-on sprint across all four lanes of Fair Street (including a nearly disastrous leap over the deepest part of the median drainage ditch) I make my way into the library, down the stairs to the basement television studio, and into the dressing room where I fully expect to find Aunt Carole harassing Dad, but he is alone, cracking his neck and rolling his shoulders and making nervous *pop-pop-pop* sounds with his lips. He wants to pace, I can tell, but the library cable access TV dressing room doubles as its prop room and there are many dusty things scattered about and precariously balanced against other dusty things. To pace would be dangerous to one's person, not to mention one's pristine Santa suit.

In the mind of a child, Santa is infallible, an ideal. They deserve that belief and a true Santa does nothing to damage it, it says in the Santa School manual. *His beard is neat and white and flawless. His boots are shined. His suit immaculate. He is perfect in appearance, in intention, in deed. Anything else sows the seed of doubt in a child. Doubt will happen eventually—do not let it begin with you.* Dad does not want a smudge on his suit or a popped button on his jacket to be the start of some kid's loss of faith. So when Dad finally notices me there in the prop room doorway, his relief is palpable. With me there, he can channel his nervous energy into talk instead of walk.

"Francie. Thank goodness," he says. "Be a kid. Ask me a question."

"Santa Claus?" I say. I'm winded and have to manage my best little-kid-on-the-phone voice between gulps of air. "How old are you?"

Dad chuckles. He has a good chuckle. An eight on a scale of ten, I think. It's warm and honest, if not magical. "Time works a little differently at the North Pole. It's the cold air, just like in your refrigerator. We stay fresher longer." Dad chuckles again. Then he pauses before he really answers. "I was around when your grandfather was a boy, and when your grandfather's grandfather was a boy, and when your grandfather's grandfather's grandfather was a boy, and many, many years before that. Now tell me, Little Emmet, have you been enjoying the holiday season?"

"I'm Little Emmet?" I ask.

"It's right there on the prompter." Dad points to an

imaginary prompter next to the imaginary camera he's been facing. The call screeners always check and double-check the kid caller's names so there is no risk Santa will mess them up. "I've always liked the name Emmet. If your brothers hadn't been twins I might have been able to convince your mother, but as soon as we knew there were two of them, they were fated for Donner and Dasher. Poor kids."

We're all of us poor kids in that respect. But I don't say that now. My job is to make things better for him, not worse. "That was good, Dad. A really good answer."

"Thanks, Francie. It was one of your Grampa's. I had almost forgotten it. Take a look at my beard, would you? I thought it felt a little shifty there for a second."

I give his whiskers a tiny tug. They are glued on good and tight. "Want another question?"

Dad nods.

"What's Mrs. Claus's name?" It's a tricky question. Mrs. Claus has had a lot of names over the last century and a half. Holly, Anna, Christine, and—thanks to Rankin and Bass, creators of the Claymation *Santa Claus Is Comin' to Town*—Jessica.

"Do you have any nicknames, Little Monica?"

"My dad calls me Monkey," I say, using my kid voice again. "And my mom calls me sweetie or honey or love when she's happy. When my room is messy I get called Monica Marie."

Seven-point chuckle. "It's the same with Mrs. Claus,"

says Dad. "We've both been around for so many years that we've had plenty of time for names and nicknames. She's been called Jessica and Anna and a lot of other things. I call her Sparkle Toes. She's a very good dancer. Now, let's talk for a minute about that bedroom of yours. How do you think it looks today, Little Monica?"

"Nice pivot," I say. I'm breathing normally now. Dad isn't, but he's less nervous than he was a few minutes ago.

"I have to use the restroom again," he tells me. "I'll meet you in the studio."

The studio is dark except for the stage. From the back of the room I can see the silhouette of the camera and of Boomer, the lady who works it. Mr. Donovan is seated in one of the two chairs on stage, talking into his phone. "Tell the grandkids I can't promise," he says. "They have the same chance for getting through as any of the Santa calls. I know I'm the head of the station, dear. Yes . . . Yes . . . Well, I wouldn't say there'd be *no* station without—it's not my—it's not my rule, dear. It's in the Santa contract. Now, we're not going to . . . You really want me to fire Santa? That's what you want to tell the grandkids, Pop-Pop fired Santa?"

"Five minutes," says Boomer. "Where's Santa?"

"He's in the restroom," I call. "He'll be right there."

"Nervous, is he?" Aunt Carole emerges from a dark studio corner. Dang, she's sneaky.

"I didn't know you were here, Aunt Carole."

She's wearing her sunglasses, like she's some Hollywood type just arriving on a movie set. Her bangles rattle as she attempts a casual wave of the hand. "This is the work of public relations, Frankincense. Media. Publicity. Image. I've looked at the past videos. The quality is remarkably poor."

Dad has come down the studio steps and is standing behind me. He looks nervous again.

"You know," Aunt Carole says to Dad, "if we took Brady up on his offer you wouldn't have to do this. He could tape the program when he was in town for Santa School. We could prerecord the show and put in some extra graphics, really glitz up the whole thing."

"Up the glitz," says Dad, though I don't think he really knows what he's saying. His eyes look nervous. His mouth looks nervous. Even his beard looks nervous.

"It's not supposed to be about glitz," I say. I can't believe she's doing this. It's like she's deliberately messing with him before he has to go on camera. "It's supposed to be real. And simple and not all flashy showmanship. It's Santa Claus, okay? It's kids calling in and talking to Santa Claus." My hands are flying in the air with every phrase. Alice says when I get mad I look like I'm tossing an invisible pizza.

"Three minutes," warns Boomer.

"Francie," says Dad, but I'm too riled up now.

"Just leave it alone, would you? Leave it like it is. Like Grampa Chris did it. This is Hollydale," I tell Aunt Carole, "not Hollywood." I fling my arm out behind me, in the direction I suppose Southern California must be. Between me and California, however, is my dad. More specifically, my dad's nose, which is famously prone to nosebleeds.

Instantly, Dad's yak-hair beard and moustache set ($549) turns scarlet.

"Dad! Are you okay?" It's the dumbest question I could ask. He's not okay. I mean, he'll be okay, but I've seen him get bloody noses before. They don't stop. Once he even had to go to Grace Memorial's urgent care. His face is suddenly pale enough to match his white gloves, or it would be if those gloves weren't covered in blood. Grampa Chris got bloody noses, too, I think, and just like that I'm remembering him, facedown in the Tree Shed—

Thankfully Aunt Carole gags, returning me to the present. "He needs to go to the doctor," I tell her. "Now."

Aunt Carole can't look at him, but she nods. "Go ahead. Take him."

Is it possible that even now, with Dad gushing blood, Aunt Carole is more interested in messing with me than she is helping out? "I can't take him," I say, struggling to keep myself from yelling. "I'm fifteen! I don't drive, remember?"

"Francie," Dad warns.

"Bryan," says Aunt Carole, and just like that Bryan appears at Aunt Carole's side. Where did she come from? "Take Santa to the hospital."

"But the show," says Dad. His voice is two parts concern to one part relief.

"I'll handle things here," says Aunt Carole. "It's local access cable. I'll tell them to put on some old basketball game."

"But," says Dad again.

"We'll reschedule. You can't go on like that."

"We'll reschedule," Dad says. He's still gushing blood and I think he might fall over. Bryan puts a stiff robotic hand on Dad's shoulder and steers him out of the studio as Aunt Carole adjusts her glasses and prepares to explain to the cable people what has happened.

"Santa on set, please," calls Boomer.

Aunt Carole strides toward the camera. "About that . . . ," she says.

"What's going on? Where's . . . ?" Pinky Donovan has just finished his call and is suddenly aware that Santa is not beside him.

"Santa on set," says Boomer again.

"Well, see, there's been a little problem," says Aunt Carole, taking a few steps closer to the camera. I don't know why, but I follow her.

"No time for problems," says Boomer.

"Unfortunately . . . ," starts Aunt Carole, but then something about the light changes and Boomer starts counting. "We're on in five, four, three . . ."

17

The familiar strains of "Santa Claus Is Coming to Town" fill the studio. There's a monitor back behind Boomer that shows what the at-home audience is seeing, *An Evening with Santa* title graphics over the image of crackling fire. A second later, the camera cuts to a close-up of station manager Pinky Donovan, who looks decidedly panicked.

"Hello . . . Hello, there Hollydale," he says. "Welcome to *An Evening with Santa*. Our annual chance to . . . uh . . . meet and talk to Santa Claus . . . live." In his panic, Mr. Donovan looks away from the camera and spots Aunt Carole pushing her silver-white hair away from her glasses. An idea forms in his station manager brain. You can see it on the monitor. It's almost violent, like he got hit in the head with a tiny snowball. His focus returns to the camera.

"Children," he says, "we have a special treat tonight—all the way from the North Pole, the one and only . . . Mrs. Claus!"

It's kind of beautiful, the panic in Aunt Carole's face just then. "He cannot mean me," she says.

"He does," I tell her.

The camera pulls back so the entire set is in view. Pinky Donovan waves one hand, pats the Santa chair with the other.

"Come on, Mrs. Claus, don't be shy. You don't want to disappoint the children."

"Yeah," I say. "You don't want to disappoint the children."

The corner of Aunt Carole's mouth curls just a little and suddenly I get it. She doesn't care about disappointing the children at all. Like Christmas train tracks clicking effortlessly together, I understand her whole nasty plan. *An Evening with Santa* is one of the best advertisements we have for Santa School. We promise media training, after all. Aunt Carole did not come to the studio to help Dad but to deliberately make him even more nervous, to make him look bad on camera. If she ruined this night, her logic must go, she could ruin school enrollment. Or at least she could make it far less likely that we'd attract new students for the school, thereby decreasing the likelihood that next year's school would break even. And, as a result, increasing the likelihood that Grampa Chris's Santa School should be franchised to Santa Slick. That I was the one who actually ruined the evening is just a bonus for her.

"Mrs. Claus?" says Mr. Donovan weakly. "For the children?

I would like to say that I am suddenly filled with the spirit of Christmas, but really I think it's the spirit of Not Letting Aunt Carole Win that has me scooping Dad's fallen Santa hat up off the studio floor. I snatch Aunt Carole's glasses from her face, too, and slam them onto my own. In an instant, I am on the stage, sunglasses darkening as I dash in front of the spotlights and slide into Santa's chair.

Mr. Donovan looks even more worried than before. "Mrs. Claus?" he squeaks. "You look a little young . . ."

He's right, of course. Now what? "No," I say, thinking fast. "Don't be silly, Mr. Donovan. I'm not Mrs. Claus."

Mr. Donovan looks me up and down, taking in my Corporate Christmas uniform. "Of course," he says, smiling. "You're . . . an elf."

An elf? No freaking way. "I'm Santa's Intern," I tell him.

You would think Pinky Donovan would be relieved by this news, but instead he looks skeptical. "Santa has interns?" he asks.

I nod as confidently as I can. "Oh, sure," I say. "It's a big operation, you know. And Santa's always happy to teach up-and-comers the ropes."

Mr. Donovan relaxes just a little, and his innate cable TV manager instincts kick into gear. If the audience is going to be satisfied with a Santa substitute, he's going to have to sell this thing. "Fascinating," he says, as if it is. "And what does an intern for Santa do?"

What does an intern for Santa do? "It depends," I say, scrambling. "Some of us are in reindeer management. Some work in gift wrap. Traffic. Coal production."

From somewhere in the studio, Aunt Carole snorts.

"I'm actually up with the top brass," I tell Mr. Donovan. "Naughty/Nice database. Gift requests."

Mr. Donovan looks at the camera. "Sounds like an important job," he says.

"It is," I say. "Santa trusts me a lot. Asks me my advice about what presents to give, which kids deserve the good stuff. You know."

I'm kind of getting into this intern thing, and Mr. Donovan is too. "So, then, Santa's Intern . . . do you have a name?"

I could come up with one, but it seems best to keep things simple. "Santa's Intern is fine," I say, tapping my sunglasses. "Best to keep incognito."

Mr. Donovan touches his earpiece and nods again. "Okay, Santa's Intern. We've got lots of children on the line. How about we take some calls?"

Take calls? I forgot about the calls!

Mr. Donovan looks at the prompter and then straight into the camera. "Our first call is from . . . Jessilyn. Jessilyn, you are on *An Evening with Santa*. Do you have a question for Santa's Intern?"

I may have prepped Dad for this event, but I've always been on the question side of things. I've never had to come up with answers. Why did I do this? *How am I supposed to know the answers?*

A tiny voice squeaks through the studio speakers. "Where is Santa?" asks Jessilyn.

"At the hospital," I say.

Mr. Donovan's pomegranate face goes white. Did I just tell a little kid that Santa's at the hospital?

"Um. Santa's at the hospital, Jessilyn, but he's just . . . there are some kids there who needed him tonight. He's making sure that they're filled with the holiday spirit. He, um, he asked me to come here and do this while he visits the sick kids."

Jessilyn sniffs and the speakers crackle. "Santa's okay?" she asks.

"Santa's fine," I tell her. "He's great."

"My grampa went to the hospital once because he had a stone inside him and he couldn't pee right."

What do you say to that? "Santa pees just fine," I tell her.

Mr. Donovan looks like he might need to visit the hospital soon too. "Jessilyn," he says quickly, "maybe you'd like to tell Santa's Intern what you want for Christmas."

"I want a phone," says Jessilyn. "A yellow phone with a cat on it, like Benjamin."

"Benjamin's your cat?" I ask.

"Benjamin's my enemy," explains Jessilyn. "He has a yellow phone with a dog on it, but cats are better."

Mr. Donovan nods, encouraging me to say yes, Santa

will bring her what she wants. But I can't say yes. When you grow up in a family like mine, one thing you know better than most people is that Santa doesn't make promises, and that you can't make promises for him. All I can do is make promises for myself.

"I will tell Santa that you and I talked, and that you asked for a phone," I say.

"You won't forget?"

"I won't forget," I tell her.

"I think you will."

This kid is persistent. "Jessilyn, I won't forget. I'd write it down if I had a pencil and paper. Mr. Donovan, do you have a pencil and paper?"

Mr. Donovan shakes his head. I suspect he is not on camera now, because he also makes a little wind-it-up motion with his fingers, but I'm not sure how to end this call. Do I just say goodbye? Tell her that time is up?

"I'm going to write you a letter and remind you," Jessilyn says.

"That's a good idea," I tell her.

"On paper," she says. "I am good at printing."

"No other way to do it," I agree. "Good old-fashioned printing on a paper letter." Mr. Donovan is tapping his watch so hard I think he'll break it. "Okay, Jessilyn. I'll watch the mail for your letter. Okay? Bye, now. Merry Christmas!"

Mr. Donovan relaxes a little when Jessilyn hangs up and we move on to the next caller. The rest of the night goes pretty well. Kids call, they ask questions. I answer. They tell me what they want and I do the Santa jujitsu I've seen demonstrated over and over at Santa School—I make no promises about what Santa will put under the tree, but assure them all that he'll do his best to make their Christmas special. The kids on the phone all sound pretty happy. By the end, I'm feeling pretty happy too. And best of all, Aunt Carole isn't.

19

Three letters arrive at the North Pole on Wednesday.

I find them in my in-box before Alice and I begin
Cookie Council. I've been putting in a lot of extra hours to
prep for Thanksgiving weekend, which is good, of course,
because I'm bringing in more Miata dollars, but it also
means that I didn't get to see Alice on Monday, and even
though we call each other and text a lot, it still feels like
we have a lot of catching up to do. She starts by asking if
I've been teased at all this week, and when I tell her a little
she tells me I need to seriously consider her plan. "The
boy doesn't have to be cute. It doesn't even need to be a
boy. All you need is someone with lips and a willingness
to use them in public."

An image of Hector Ramirez leaning over to not-kiss

me during Mythology Today floats into my brain, but I push it away. Hector Ramirez is not interested in me. And even if he was, what would I do then? My daydream self may be an accomplished kisser, but the real-life Francie?

"There are no boys," I tell Alice.

I take a bite of oatmeal raisin cookie to stall for time. I'd really rather talk about her life or, even better, about stupid nothing stuff, like we used to do when we both went to Our Lady of Sorrows. It was easy then, because we had all the same classes and knew all the same people and saw all the same things. We'd experience everything together and we knew each other well enough to know what we thought about those things without discussing them in detail. Our time together was about ignoring the rest of our lives, going to the library or riding our bikes up and down Santa Claus Lane or drawing or singing along to the radio or playing Christmas-opoly. (Alice was always the stocking. I chose the sleigh.)

Now catching up is required to keep us connected, and yet *having* to catch up feels like proof of how far apart our lives are, and how important earning my Miata money has become. Even so, I'd rather not talk about all of this right now. I pick up one of the letters I've taken from my in-box and open it, hoping to divert Alice's attention.

Dear Intern, it says. *My name is Katie Culp. I live in Hollydale. I have been very good this year. Please tell Santa I want glitter pens and a phone and glitter shoes too. They have those at Target.*

Thank you and Merry Christmas.
    Katie

The letter is neatly written in pencil and includes a crayon drawing of what I assume is Katie wearing glitter shoes.

"That is *so* cute," said Alice. "I want glitter shoes too."

"Who doesn't want glitter shoes?" I reply, but instantly I look over my shoulder in case Bryan is around. Glitter shoes may be part of my next uniform and I don't want her to have ammunition. My current uniform, the one I've been wearing since Monday, is a take on the athleisure trend—a garnet-colored track suit with TEAM SANTA printed in white letters on the back of the jacket. It actually wouldn't be that bad if it didn't also require me to wear a green and white sweatband around my head. Still, it is the most comfortable and least embarrassing uniform so far, and while I wouldn't want Bryan or Aunt Carole to think I'm happy about it, I'm actually planning to give it decent marks. If we *had* to wear some kind of uniform on the salesfloor, this wouldn't be the worst option.

I open the other two letters. They're equally adorable. Cyrus Magoon has not hit his sister in three weeks and wants an Xbox. Serafina Lee wants a sled and a bike and a helmet that matches both. That letter ends by telling me how pretty I looked on the TV and asking me to write back if I can.

"Smart kid, flattering the intern," says Alice. "That's how you get things done."

"Too bad robots are impervious to flattery," I say. "I'd try it with Bryan."

And then, as if the mention of her name has activated a homing device, Bryan is in the doorway of the breakroom.

"You found the letters," she says.

"It didn't take much searching," I tell her. "They were in my in-box."

"It often takes you several days to find the memos we put there, so I couldn't be sure." Squint. She explains that the cable station put up their address at the end of the broadcast. "These letters were delivered there before being forwarded to us, so already there has been some delay on your part."

"On my part? I read them as soon as I got them," I say. "What do you want me to do, anyway, call Santa Claus and tell him about the Xbox?"

"*I* don't want you to do anything. *Carole* requests that you write replies."

"She requests, does she? You know what I request— Ouch!" Alice is crushing my foot under her Regina, Queen of Heaven saddle shoe. "Mi-a-ta," she mouths.

Bryan smug-squints. "You request?"

Dang. What could I request? "Um. Stationery," I say. "North Pole stationery. You know, so the letter looks official."

It takes Bryan's microchip brain a second to process

that there is nothing snotty in my statement. "Hm," she says. "Not a bad idea."

"Maybe even an idea that shows Initiative?" I say. "And Creative Problem Solving?" Why not get some Pillar Points while I can?

"I'll get back to you," she says, and then she's gone.

Alice takes a sip from her "You'd Better Watch Out" mug. "Quick thinking. But now you have to answer the letters."

"Maybe. Maybe she and Aunt Carole will forget everything once they have to invest their own time in finding stationery." I take another bite of cookie. "Besides, it's only three letters. 'Dear Katie: Thanks for writing. I'm forwarding your request to Santa. Please continue being good. Have a great Christmas! Love, Santa's Intern.' Done."

"You aren't going to mention the drawing? It's a great drawing. Look at the sparkle rays shooting off those shoes."

"'PS: You are quite an artist!'" I say. "Done again."

"Very nice," says Alice. "If only you would apply those keen creative problem-solving skills to the kissing issue, your life would be perfect. Now tell me about what's been going on at school."

20

The Friday after Thanksgiving is always super busy at the Hollydale Holiday Shop and this year is no exception. I spend most of my time on the salesfloor, helping customers and restocking ornaments and trying to keep my uniform sweatband from dropping down over my eyes. On breaks, I head to Snowflake where it is quiet and, coincidentally, the windows offer a view of the Library Fundraising Christmas Tree Lot across the street, where it just so happens that a fine-shouldered Hector Ramirez is among the volunteers. Few things will lift the spirits like watching a cute guy lift a tree. Plus, he seems to be pretty good at it, at least as far as little kids are concerned. The library lot is too far away for me to make out anyone's faces, but I've seen enough kids dancing around in a Santa line to recognize pure joy when I see it, and when Hector straps a pine to the top of a Subaru, well, the kid dancing says it all.

Breaks aside, it is a long day. By the time Mom makes the announcement that the shop is closing for the night, I am beat. Normally I'd wait around for Dad or Mom if they are closing, or I'd just walk home, but tonight I'm headed to the North Pole to drop off my uniform and evaluation sheet. It's not due to Aunt Carole until Saturday afternoon, but I want to follow up on my outstanding Creative Problem Solving and Initiative moments and scoop up another Pillar Point for Timeliness and Responsibility while I'm in good favor, so I've filled it out neatly and fully.

UNIFORM EVALUATION #4:

TEAM SANTA

Breathability: 7 (unless you count sweatband, which actually CAUSED me to sweat and gets a 0).

Cleanability: 10. Washed well. Even coffee stains came out no problem.

Durability: 8.

Visibility: 8.

Restriction of Movement: None that I noticed. In fact, pants could have been a little smaller.

Comments: I know I've been resistant to all of these uniforms and I still think the shop doesn't need them, but if you're going to force people to wear some kind of outfit, this is the least awful so far.

When I get to the second floor, I have second thoughts. Aunt Carole is usually long gone by six o'clock, but there is a light on in her office. She's on her phone and I can hear her bracelets rattling.

"Just print it," she demands. "It's a community paper and I am an important member of this community. This shop spends a lot of advertising dollars with your little birdcage liner, you know." Rattle. Rattle.

I suspect she's talking to someone from the *Hollydale Daily*, the weekly paper that Alice hopes to get a story in this year. (It used to be a daily back before the internet killed most newspapers. They switched to a weekly about ten years ago, but never got around to switching the name.) The shop places a lot of ads during the season and there are always a couple of stories about trends in holiday decor or our annual Christmas Eve party. My guess is that Aunt Carole is railing about that, hoping to get some early press coverage.

I turn around as slowly and quietly as I can. I'll just drop my evaluation form in her in-box. She might not notice it until Monday, which isn't as good as having it on her desk for Bryan to find tomorrow morning, but it's better than actually having to talk to Aunt Carole.

"Stop," says Aunt Carole.

Dang! I freeze, then turn around, nearly falling over a cardboard box that has no reason to be sitting where it is.

Fortunately, Aunt Carole's command was not to me but to the person on the telephone. Unfortunately, my abrupt halting and rotating and near box-falling has attracted her attention. She rattle-waves me into her office.

"I don't need your warnings. Just print it." She hangs up the phone. "Frankincense," she says. "What are you doing up here so late?"

"I have my evaluation form," I say. "I'm turning it in early, which you might notice demonstrates great Timeliness and Responsibility."

"Your what? Oh. Your form. We won't be needing those anymore."

Is she kidding? I've filled out the form. I've been Timely and Responsible. On the other hand . . . "So, we're done with the whole uniform testing thing? Which one did you pick?" *Please don't let it be Cowboy Christmas.*

"Did you really think we'd be ordering any of those fancy uniforms for the entire staff? Please. Not with our margins."

Now she *has* to be kidding. "Are you kidding?" I ask. "For four weeks I've looked like a Christmas idiot for nothing?"

"Not for nothing. Bryan got extra credit in her marketing course," says Aunt Carole.

"Oh, well, that was worth it," I say. Aunt Carole ignores my sarcasm and holds out her hand for the evaluation form, which I give her. I'm still fuming, but I'm also starting to realize that this means I really am done with the uniforms. I can wear my regular clothes and stop being polite to tourists who want me to bend over. I repeat myself, this time trying to erase the sarcasm. There still might be a chance for some Pillar Points if I get gracious about this. "If it helps Bryan, then it was worth it," I say. "Although I am glad to hear that I'm done with the uniforms. I don't know that any of them really represented the shop and what we're all about and—"

"You're not done with the uniforms," she says.

What? "But you just said you aren't considering shop uniforms. You said you don't need any more evaluations."

Aunt Carole smiles a Grinchy sort of smile. "That is true. The shop doesn't need a uniform. But *you* do. You are Santa's Intern, after all."

She holds out a copy of this week's *Hollydale Daily News*. On the front page is a photo of me, lifted from *An Evening with Santa*. I'm in my Corporate Christmas uniform, suspenders crossed over my chest, Dad's Santa hat pulled down over my ears, and darkened sunglasses covering half my face.

SANTA'S INTERN WANTS YOUR LETTERS says the headline. I start to read the article, but apparently Aunt Carole doesn't have time for that. "You made promises," she says, folding the paper in half. "Those promises reflect on this store. Now you need to keep them."

"I told Bryan I'd write those kids back as soon as I had some stationery."

"Have you looked in your in-box?"

I haven't. Dang. "The stationery is there?"

"An entire box. The invitations department designed and printed it up just for you."

"I don't need a whole box," I tell her. "There are only three letters."

"There *were* only three letters," says Aunt Carole.

"Did we get more?"

"Check your in-box, Frances."

I go downstairs and check my in-box. As promised, it contains a large package of stationery. Letterhead, actually. A Santa hat and a pair of sunglasses form a little logo, under which it says,

OFFICE OF SANTA CLAUS

Santa's Intern

c/o Hollydale Holiday Shop

and the store address. It's pretty sharp, I have to admit. I'll bet Mom designed it herself. I take the stationery out of my in-box and look for the other letters Aunt Carole implied would be there. There are no other letters. There is, however, a piece of notebook paper with Bryan's robotic printing on it: *See Carole in Marketing.*

I just saw Carole in Marketing. But fine. I go back upstairs to see Aunt Carole. "Did you go to your in-box?" she asks.

I hold up the letterhead as proof that I have in fact followed her directions. "And there was a note from Bryan saying to see you."

Aunt Carole nods.

"I was just up here," I remind her.

"I know," says Aunt Carole. She is loving this.

"Okay. I'm here. I see you. Now what?"

Aunt Carole rattles in the direction of the box I tripped over earlier. "Open it."

I open the box. Inside must be fifty letters, all addressed to Santa's Intern. "Holy moly," I say. I mean, I didn't even know that many kids actually watched *An Evening with Santa*. It's on local access cable, after all.

"They need to be responded to in a Timely Manner," says Aunt Carole. I swear I can hear the capital *T* in *timely*.

"When? I'm scheduled to work the salesfloor tomorrow," I tell her.

"Bryan will make sure your Intern uniform is here before you clock in. We'd like you to wear it whenever you're working. It's good marketing. And you can write your letters on Sunday."

"I have plans on Sunday," I tell her. Alice and I are going to the mall. The stores are going to be crazy on Thanksgiving weekend, and even though you'd think I'd be sick of the retail frenzy, I kind of love the energy of it as long as I am not the one working.

Aunt Carole shrugs. She's more skilled at sarcasm than I am. Even her shoulders have it. "I expect you'll have the ingenuity to figure something out." She picks up the *Hollydale Daily* again. "Amazing how they can take a still image right off the video like that, isn't it?"

"Amazing," I say.

"Bryan knows how to do that too," she says. She lifts a piece of printer paper which also holds a picture of me taken straight from video. Surveillance video. It's not in color like the newspaper photo, but it is a miraculously sharp image, sharp enough to make out all the important details, including which of my five fingers I am using to communicate with Sam Spinek.

"You're going to put that in my file for Dad, aren't you? You're going to dock my Pillar Points." The truth is at this moment I don't care about Pillar Points and salary raises and the Miata. I care about my dad. I really don't want him seeing this photo. I don't want him to fight with Aunt Carole about it. He's working hard enough. And, well, as much as it doesn't seem very teenagery to admit it, I care a lot about what my dad thinks of me. And I don't want him thinking of me like this. Like someone who would do this in the middle of the family shop.

"I haven't quite figured out which file it belongs in. I'm still deciding." She dangles the paper over her trash can, then moves it to hover over an open file on her desk. Trash can, file, trash can, file.

"Ingenuity," I say. "I'm on it."

21

I bring the stationery and the box of letters home with me, dropping them heavily on the kitchen table. Dad is in the kitchen tidying up after Don and Dash, who made some sort of chocolate milkshake concoction before they headed off to bed.

"Are those the Santa letters?" asks Dad.

I nod. "Aunt Carole says I have to answer them all."

"I know," says Dad. "Want some tea?"

I do. Dad puts on the kettle and busies himself pulling mugs and spoons and sugar from their various drawers and cabinets. "She's right, you know." He says this without looking at me. "We owe the kids responses."

"But why do I have to be the one to respond? I know I told kids to send letters, but it's not like I *really* work for

Santa Claus. Anybody could write back. Bryan could do it."

"Bryan is your aunt's intern. And I don't know how much she really understands about who we are and what we do. We can't have just anyone respond. We have great people working here, Francie. They're loyal and well-intentioned, but when it comes to Santa we have to be really careful." He quotes the line from the Santa School manual about not sowing the seeds of doubt for children. "There aren't a lot of people I trust to get this exactly right." He counts the people on his fingers. "Me. Your mom. Maybe Kelly in Nativity. Jerry in Receiving. And you."

"Then why can't—" I start, but Dad cuts me off.

"This is peak season. All those people are essential to running the shop. Every one of us is going to be working double- , maybe triple-time to get orders out and help customers and do the restocking. They won't have any extra hours to give. The only person I have available to me is you."

"So I'm not essential," I say. Which is stupid. Of course I'm not essential. I may know the store better than most, but I'm not the worker that most of our long-time employees are. I can call in sick and be easily replaced.

Dad lifts the kettle off the stove a second before it whistles.

"Okay, but Dad, when am I supposed to do this? I'm scheduled to work almost thirty hours next week and I have homework and I don't want to miss hanging out with Alice."

"Peppermint or ginger?" Dad asks. I take ginger. It feels less overtly Christmassy.

"I can't do anything about your homework, but I'll see what I can do about your shop schedule. And I'll make sure you get paid for any time you spend on this. Like you said, you're not a real intern."

I perk up a little. "Paid how much?" I ask, ready to do the Miata calculations.

"Anything beyond your scheduled store hours will have to come out of the marketing budget. I'll check with Carole." He sets my tea in front of me and sits down with his own. "Did you see the newspaper?" he asks.

"I saw the front-page picture," I tell him. "I didn't read the article."

Dad puts a hand on my shoulder. "It's a nice article. You should read it. You did a great job covering for me, Francie. I'm proud of you."

"Thank you," I say. I sip my tea and try to hide how much it matters to me that he's proud. I'm a teenager, right? I'm not supposed to care about such things. "I'm not sure Aunt Carole thought it was a nice article. I overheard her on the phone arguing with someone from the paper. She must have written a response, because she was demanding that they print something she'd sent them."

Dad winces. "Are you sure that's what you heard?"

I tell him I'm sure.

"Martha?" he calls to my mother. "Do you have the newspaper?"

Dad heads to the living room for the paper and I am left alone with my tea and the box of Intern letters.

So many letters, all from kids who deserve the kind of response Grampa Chris would give them.

I sip my ginger tea, and just like that, I'm back in Snowflake listening to Grampa Chris talk with a class of Santas. "What do you do," asks one of the new students, "when a kid asks for something you know they aren't going to get?"

The questioner, I'm sure, was thinking about things like race cars or ponies, but Grampa Chris knew that pony requests weren't the most difficult ones his Santas would face. I watched his face soften, his hand find something in his jacket pocket.

Once, Grampa Chris told them, a little girl sat on his lap and told him that her mother was sick and in the hospital. The doctors were saying that her mother was going to die. *Santa,* said the girl, *what I want for Christmas is for you to make my mom not die.*

Snowflake got quiet then. Grampa Chris let it be quiet. He let the little girl and her Christmas wish take hold of them. He let them feel her weight on their own knees, hear her voice in their ears.

"What do you say to that?" asked a student Santa. One of the younger guys. Thick dark hair. Only the beginnings of a paunch.

Grampa Chris let the young Santa's question fill the quiet too. Then he said, "Santa is an idea. An ideal. He is magic, but he can't do magic. He doesn't make promises that might not be kept. Even for simple things like a baseball or a coloring book. We can't know the circumstances of the children who come to us. There are only two things we can truly give a child. Our attention and our love."

Some of the Santas nodded. Many of them had been to Santa School before and they knew this story, but they still felt the importance of what Grampa Chris had said as if it were the first time they'd heard it.

But there were new Santas there too. "But what do you say?" one of them asked. "What do you say to that?"

"You'll figure it out," said Grampa Chris.

This answer didn't satisfy everyone. It didn't satisfy me, either, and I couldn't help myself. Even though I wasn't a student, I raised my hand.

Grampa Chris smiled in my direction. "Francie?"

"What did *you* say?" I asked him. "What did you say to that girl?"

Grampa Chris nodded then. He knew that my question was shared by many of the Santas too. Santas want answers. Everyone wants answers. "I keep a little book with me when I'm working," he said, and then he fished a notebook out of his pocket. It was small, maybe four inches tall, with a leather cover and a little leather loop that held a tiny pencil. "I wrote down the little girl's name. I let her watch me do it. I wrote *Laura's Mom*. And then I promised to pray for her."

"That's it?" says a student Santa. "You tell her you'll pray?"

"No," said Grampa Chris. "Then I keep my promise."

22

NOVEMBER 26

As it turns out, I am not the only person in Hollydale offended by the shiny silver wreath Aunt Carole insisted on hanging on the North Pole front door.

It seems that as winter approaches and the sky has begun to darken during what passes for Hollydale's rush hour, the wreath's shiny silver surface has been catching the headlights of passing cars, giving off a vibe that is less Traditional Midwestern Christmas and more New Year's Rockin' Eve. The disco wreath, as one of the two *Hollydale Daily* letter-to-the-editor writers calls it, is not only "ugly" and "an affront" and "all that is wrong with liberal America," but, says this concerned citizen, could, under the right conditions, become a driving hazard. "Pointy death rays of light" might temporarily blind a passing motorist, says the letter, and result in tragedy.

The first letter was published under the pseudonym "Blinded by the Light," but the second, which displays a strikingly similar tone, if intensified vocabulary, was signed by "Concerned Citizen Melanie Stebanow." It was the signatory that had really gotten to Aunt Carole, Dad explained. The Concerned Citizen was her rival back in their high school days, and according to my aunt, maintains a grudge today. Apparently she, Carole, was thought by people in the know to have been next in line to make homecoming court during their senior year, while Melanie was only next-next. Besides, Aunt Carole told Dad, she had been assured by her book club that most of Hollydale adores the new wreath and thinks it gives life to what had been a dull and predictable display.

This, more or less, was what Aunt Carole told Dad she intended to submit as a response to the *Hollydale Daily*. Even though Dad asked her not to.

Which is why she is mad at him.

Which is why, when he went to talk with her about getting some marketing department funds for the time I will have to spend writing letters to kids, Aunt Carole came up with an even fouler plan.

On the Hollydale Holiday Shop salesfloor, tucked between the Stationery department and the nativity sets, is a massive antique desk that once belonged to my great-grandfather. Usually, the desk displays the sort of Victorian holiday cards that are favored by old ladies and people whose Netflix queues are stuffed with Jane Austen movies. Now, however, the desk has a bright green mailbox on it, the words *Santa's Intern* painted on the side in gaudy gold lettering.

"Don't touch it," says Bryan. "The paint is a little tacky." I resist the urge to agree.

During my hours in the shop, Bryan informs me, I am to sit at the desk in my intern uniform, answering the children's letters. "This way, you can still be on the salesfloor and can direct customers as needed, but you can also be writing to the children. It's true retail-tainment," she explains as she hands me my Corporate Christmas uniform. It is also a way to make sure that I don't get any extra pay for my letter-writing time.

I go to the restroom to change. There is a note pinned to the suspenders, reminding me to wear them backward as I did on *An Evening with Santa*. She has even tucked Aunt Carole's sunglasses into the breast pocket of my Corporate Christmas dress shirt. When I return to meet Bryan on the salesfloor, there is a full box of letters on the desk with at least a hundred envelopes inside. "Where did these come from?" I ask.

"Children," says Bryan.

"I know they came from children," I say. "But how did there get to be so many? There were around fifty yesterday."

"I believe the newspaper coverage encouraged more children to write. Either that, or the posting on YouTube."

"On YouTube?"

"YouTube is a remarkably powerful video platform where people and corporations share—"

"I know what YouTube is, Bryan. I don't know what YouTube has to do with these letters."

"Given the response to your appearance on the local show, Carol and I thought that we should maximize exposure. There really aren't that many views of the video, but those we do have seem to be prompting a good response." She points an android finger at the boxes, as if I'm too dim to make the connection for myself. I can make the connection. What I can't make is enough time to answer all those letters, especially not while sitting at a desk in the middle of the shop where people I know might be able to watch me like I'm some kind of street mime. I'll quit first. Even the Miata is not worth this. I'm about to tell her so when this tiny boy walks up to the desk.

"Do you work for Santa?" he says. He has big eyes, this kid. They take up half his face.

"I'm an intern," I say. I shoot a look at Bryan. "I don't really do that much work."

"But you work for Santa?" he says again. You can hear the hope in his voice. He's a full-on Santa Claus believer.

I can almost hear my Grampa Chris reading from the manual. *Doubt will happen eventually. Do not let it begin with you.*

"Yes," I tell him. "I work for Santa."

The kid keeps looking at me with those eyes. He doesn't move away, but he doesn't say anything else either.

"Is there something you want me to tell Santa?" I prompt.

The kid doesn't say anything for a second. Then he says, "Tell him that I want to be his intern when I'm your age."

Bryan squints at me. She thinks she has me pinned. She thinks there is no way I will walk away from this kid and all the kids like him that have written these letters. She believes that there is no way I will ruin their Santa faith.

She's right.

I sit down at the desk. I take up the pen. "What's your name, kiddo? I'll see to it that Santa knows."

Dear Damon:

Thanks for your letter. I'm glad to hear you have been good this year. I'll make sure to tell Santa about the yellow bike with orange flames and wheels that make real smoke. I'm sure Santa will do his best to make your holiday special.

Dear Laurel:

Santa is grateful for the reminder of how much better lavender purple is than grape purple, especially for winter coats.

Dear Mickey:

Santa has not yet read those books about
the time-traveling rescue dog, but he is glad
to have your recommendation.

Thanks to years of collating the manual, listening in on Santa School classes, and watching Grampa Chris in action, I understand the rules.

Never make promises for Santa, other than that he will do his best.

If there is any way to let the parent know what the child has asked for, do so.

Never use a child's name unless you are absolutely certain you have it right.

And most important, never be the seed of doubt.

Because of the limited spelling and penmanship skills of my correspondents, I have to resort to addressing some of them as "Dear Kiddo" or "Dear Friend," and sometimes I don't repeat the list of things they want because I can't be sure if they're asking for a doll or a ball. But mostly, the responses are simple and I can move through them pretty quickly.

Periodically, families and small groups of tourists gather to watch me write. Sometimes they ask questions about what it is like to work for Santa or if I've met Mrs. Claus or where the restrooms are located. There's no security camera for this part of the store, so Bryan stops by several times to "observe," scratching comments in her notebook and snapping photos for the store Instagram.

Between talking with customers and adjusting my suspenders, I complete twenty-one letters before my break. By my calculations, I should get through half of the letters by the end of today and can finish up on my after-school shifts on Tuesday and Thursday. Then, even if I have to keep wearing this stupid outfit, I can at least go back to being a regular salesclerk and not have Bryan and Carole watching my every move.

After a cup of coffee and a peanut butter cookie, I return to my desk. Someone, Bryan presumably, has taken the finished letters away and has replenished my stack of Santa's Intern letterhead. She's also reorganized the desk, lining up the pens in a smug little row. Done by Thursday, I remind myself.

I reach under the desk and into what should be a half empty box of Letters to Santa's Intern, but Bryan seems to have reorganized things there, too. I poke my head underneath the desk. The box is full again. More than full. There are letters spilling out onto the floor.

I lift my head just in time for Bryan to snap another photo. "You're going to need to pick up the pace a little," she says.

23

BY THE END OF THE NIGHT

My hand aches. There are ink stains on my Corporate Christmas shirt. I have written ninety-seven letters to the children of Hollydale and surrounding areas.

I have acknowledged requests for electronics, bicycles, dolls, art supplies, clothes, remote control vehicles, action figures, board games, and sporting equipment, plus an archery set (not plastic), two ballet dancer outfits (one pink, one unspecified), a horse, a monkey, a kitten (white with a black spot), and at least a dozen puppies. I text Alice about it but my thumbs are even more clumsy than usual after a day of handwriting.

When did kids start loving poppies? she asks.

Shoot. Not poppies. Poopies.

Poopies? That's a crappy gift.

Poppies.

Dogs.

Smell dogs.

Small.

Puppies! texts Alice. Put me down for one too. A puppy and some sparkle shoes.

You got it, I tell her.

Do you still want to go shopping tomorrow? Or will you be working?

No work. But no shop, ok? I'm tired. You come here?

Excellent, Tarzan. I'll come there.

Donut mock me, I warn.

Sorry. I'll meet you after Mass and we can go to your house. But only if I can read some of the poopy letters.

Deal.

24

Today it's just Mom and Don and Dash and me at church and Mom is in such a hurry to get back to the shop we're out of the pew before the recessional begins. "Find Alice and let's go," she whispers.

Mom drops Don and Dash at our house with Gram and then heads for work. Alice and I walk with her part of the way and then veer off toward the North Pole in search of cookies and puppy letters.

When I was done with my shift yesterday, I took the box of yet-to-be-replied-to letters to Snowflake. I also borrowed a file about the history of Christmas parades for my Mythology Today exploration. The Hollydale Christmas parade is next Saturday. Uncle Jack will drive the flatbed truck that pulls the trailer for the mechanical reindeer and Dad's Santa sleigh.

The reindeer have been through a lot in the last few years. Grampa Chris was great at maintaining them, but Dad's been so busy with the financial part of the shop that he hasn't had time to be as diligent. After the parade, Uncle Jack plans to take the team apart and drive Rudolph and a couple of the other deer to Peoria to a guy who can strengthen their necks and correct the circuitry for Rudolph's nose. Uncle Jack's worried—reasonably, I think—that there is some danger of the nose shorting out and catching fire, which would likely change the parade experience for most viewers.

Alice is impressed by the number of letters I've received. "I didn't know there were this many kids in Hollydale," she says.

"Not all of them are Hollydale," I tell her. "I've seen some from Muncie and Naperville and even Terre Haute."

"Can I read one?" asks Alice, rifling through the box.

"Sure," I say. "Just be careful not to tear the return address when you open it."

Alice rubs her hands together gleefully, opens an envelope, and reads:

> *Dear Santa's Intern:*
>
> *I hear you know Santa really well. Could you tell him not to bring me any pants this year? Two times already this year I asked*

for a paintball gun and two times I didn't
get one, but I did get pants. Pants are not a
good gift. Except for one time during recess,
I have been pretty good this year and I
already said sorry and Henry said okay.
　　Your friend,
　　Logan

"I love this letter," says Alice. "Can I keep it?"

I shake my head. "The shop's keeping them. We're going to use them for Santa training next year."

"Well, can I answer it? Can I write back?" She's got Logan's letter pressed to her chest. "Please?"

"I don't know. It's kind of tricky."

"Please-please?"

Even though her eyebrows are doing crazy things, I can tell she's really serious about this. "Tell me what you'd say."

"Okay." Alice thinks for a second. "'Dear Logan—'"

"Good start."

"'Thank you for your letter. I do know Santa very well and he is a lovely person. You'd like him.'"

"You're taking too long. We've got a lot of letters here."

"Okay. Sorry. Um. 'I will remind Santa of your interest in the paintball gun as well as your disinterest in adding to your supply of pants.'"

"Not bad. Now, don't make any promises, but give the kid hope."

"'I'm sure that Santa will get you just the right thing this year—'"

"Nope. What if he doesn't? What if there are more pants?"

"Okay. Um. 'Santa has a lot of kids to worry about so sometimes he can't get everybody everything they ask for—'"

"Santa doesn't worry," I tell her.

"No? Okay. This is harder than I thought. 'Santa will . . .'"

"Do his best," I tell her.

"'Santa will do his best . . . to make your Christmas merry.'"

"Okay. And?"

"'And I'm glad that Henry forgave you. Sounds like a good friend.'"

"Personal. That's nice. Now wrap it up."

"Um. . . . 'Keep on being good—'"

"Implied coal threat. Try again."

"'Merry Christmas! Santa's Intern.'"

"Excellent. Yes. You may write that letter," I tell her.

I give Alice a sheet of Santa's Intern letterhead and she starts her Logan letter. As long as she is at it, I might as well answer a letter too. I might not get paid for my time, but it is one less letter I'll have to write in front of the crowds at the salesfloor intern desk.

It's quiet and comfortable writing like this. It reminds me of how we used to sit in Alice's kitchen and color in coloring books. We didn't need to talk or have the computer on or anything. We were both just coloring and in our own worlds, but together. It feels like there are fewer opportunities to do stuff like that now that we are in high school.

"Can I do another?" she asks.

I know that Dad said I was the only one who could do the job, but Alice is pretty good and I won't let anything go out that I wouldn't write myself. "Sure, but tell me what you're going to say before you write it."

By the fourth letter, Alice is a pro. We spend an hour writing before we break for cookies. We eat those in the breakroom, away from the letters. Chocolate fingerprints are not exactly faith-inspiring.

There are some other employees in the breakroom when we first get there, but by the time we pour our coffee, they're putting their employee aprons on and heading back to Ornaments.

"So, what's going on with—" Alice sticks her tongue out at me.

"They're still at it. Not a lot. Not even every day. But every time I kind of forget about it, Gunther or one of his fellow puckheads will show up and—" I don't even know how to describe it. I mean, it feels so ridiculous to even care. Sticking out your tongue is like a third-grade thing. Nobody older than nine would be bothered by it.

So how come I am bothered? How come every single time I feel this humiliating shame? It's stupid. It's ridiculous. But it's real, the shame. And it isn't because when I was thirteen I was so naive and inexperienced that I had no idea how kissing worked. It is because I still don't. Because, I am certain, I never will. Because no matter how much I like a boy, I will never risk feeling that stupid again.

I'm thinking this. I'm thinking about how I will never, ever kiss a boy and suddenly I'm picturing the fine-shouldered Hector Ramirez.

"What," says Alice, "were you just thinking? You were thinking about my plan, weren't you?"

Her PDA plan. No, I wasn't. But I don't want to tell her about Hector, either, because she'll get just as giddy about Hector as she did about writing that first Santa's Intern letter.

I make a conversational pivot. "You know, Sam Spinek had the same idea you did."

"You talked to him? You actually got up the guts and talked to him? Francie, I am so proud!" She says this last part all motherly and fake-teary.

"He talked to me." I tell her about him being in the store and filling out the evaluation and how he stood there and gave me a hard time. I can feel my face grow crimson as I speak.

"You like him," Alice sings in a little-kid-teasing way.

"I don't," I tell her. In movies and TV shows, the best friend always says this kind of thing and the audience knows that the best friend is right, but Alice is not right.

Alice just likes intrigue. And singing. "The only thing I like is the possibility that if I DID kiss him I might get it right this time and then he'd have to shut up and tell his band of merry man-children to shut up too."

"That sounds like a good reason to me," says Alice.

"It is not a good reason," I say. I mean it. Because if I do kiss right, I do not want to be kissing Sam Spinek. And if I kiss wrong, I don't want it to be him either.

25

NOVEMBER 28

Because we missed two days of school last week, we are told that last Friday is now this Monday, and as a result I am starting first period in Mythology Today. Ms. Colando (blue T-shirt with Wonder Woman punching a Nazi on it) has put us in our groups again. Ellie is going on about *Heathers* which, she would like us to know, was made in 1988 and presents a version of teenage social structures that is more *Lord of the Flies* than *Lord of the Rings*. I don't know what she means by this. Both seem pretty violent.

"It's not about the violence," she says. "It is about how social groups are structured and what holds them together. The mythology of *Lord of the Rings* suggests these groups are united by a common understanding of good and evil, that a small group of people united for good can overcome whatever unthinking, hoardish evil the world puts forth."

"People and elves," says Hector.

Elves. I shudder.

"Are you cold?" asks Hector. "I have a jacket."

A jacket suited for those amazingly perfect shoulders. "Um. No, thank you."

"People. Elves. Hobbits. Et cetera," says Ellie. "In fact, that makes my point all the more. The *Heathers*-slash-*Lord of the Flies* value system cannot posit a world with any believable unity of different classes, races, or interests united for good. Remember Martha Dunstock?"

I have seen *Heathers*. Martha Dunstock used to be friends with one of the Heathers, but got ditched when the Heather got popular and started dressing like the other girls did.

"*Lord of the Flies* is more about forming bonds for self-preservation and that these bonds are only as strong as our self-interest," says Ellie.

She'd go on, but Ms. Colando interrupts to say that we have only five minutes of class time left and we should finish our discussions.

DeKieser goes next. "My last, like, exploration or whatever was about the whole college brochures thing. My brother, Lincoln, is getting, like, stacks of them and they all kind of look, like, the same or whatever even though each one says they are, like, distinct and unique and the very best place for the individual he is and stuff. So that's, like, an opposition and, like, I'm kind of analyzing that."

Despite the *whatever*s and the *like*s, DeKieser's exploration sounds super smart and I tell her so.

"Thanks," she says.

The bell rings before Hector or I get our turn, which doesn't bother me too much because I have been so busy writing letters to Santa that I haven't been able to think about writing anything else. But then Hector says how he'd like to talk out his subject a little and maybe we could find some time to do that together.

And just like that—knees wobble, heart booms, hair at the base of neck prickles. "Yes," I say, because it is a short word and longer words would take more focus than my brain currently has available.

"You live by your family's Christmas store, right?" he says in his rumbly voice-over voice. It is the voice of the movie of my dreams. *In a world where girls know how to kiss* . . .

"Yes," I say again.

"My brother and I are working the charity Christmas Tree Lot at the library," he says. I try to make my face look like I haven't noticed this, like I haven't stood at the window of Snowflake watching Hector in the library lot filling his arms with twine-bound trees and feeling, for the first time in my life, weirdly jealous of a blue spruce. "I'll be there this afternoon. Maybe we could meet on my break?"

"Yes." I need to add longer words. "Yes, we could do that." Still all single syllables, but at least one of them has five letters.

"Should I come to you?"

"Yes. You should come to me." Oh, idiocy. Focus. "I've got some work I'm doing at the North Pole—that's the house that faces the road, across from the library. The one with the disco wreath? I mean, *we* don't call it the disco wreath, it's really called the Silver Shimmer Wreath and it costs about three hundred dollars, if you can believe that." Am I really quoting him merchandise prices? What is wrong with me?

"So I should meet you there?"

"Yes. Come around the back of the building to where the staff entrance is. There's almost always someone there and they'll tell you where to find me."

"Okay," says Hector. He slides his arms into the jacket I should have said yes to borrowing and shrugs it up over his mighty fine shoulders. "I'll see you then."

"Yes," I say. "Yes."

26

I said yes. Why did I say yes?

I said yes, I tell myself, because a reasonable person, when asked to discuss a homework issue and only a homework issue, says yes. She says yes and then she does not obsess about why she said yes through an entire day's worth of classes and a bus ride home. She does not stand around waiting for her best friend's bus in front of a reflective holiday wreath, checking to make sure that her mascara looks okay in case that homework person comes over right away. She does not stare pathetically at the Library Fundraising Christmas Tree Lot and then pretend she is not staring pathetically at the Library Fundraising Christmas Tree Lot and then stare all over again at the Library Fundraising Christmas Tree Lot as she waits for her best friend to get off the interfaith party bus.

A reasonable person does not worry about these things because she knows that this boy of the shoulders and the loanable jacket and the movie voice-over voice is not interested in Francie Time. He is interested in his homework. And getting a decent grade. And going to college far, far away from girls who are hoping that maybe somehow in the middle of talking about their homework he will develop a sudden desire to kiss them.

And besides, I don't want him to kiss me.

I mean.

Well.

I text Alice that I might have to talk homework with a classmate for a few minutes while she's here.

Actually, I text that I might have to **talk ham work** with a classmate, but she gets what I mean.

A boy? she asks. **Anyone special? Does he have lips?**

I shove my phone in my coat pocket without answering. *It got too cold for texting* is what I'll tell her, because it did. There still isn't any snow on the ground, but winter is here. I can see puffs of breath coming from the workers at the tree lot across the street. There are at least five of them this afternoon, all wearing knit hats and flannel shirts like the one Paul Bunyan wore in the *American Myths and Tall Tales* book that Ms. Colando showed us. You would think this uniform would make it difficult to discern which of the be-flanneled is Hector, but his shoulders are a giveaway, even from one hundred yards.

He and the other Bunyonites are unloading a truck full of trees, all of which are bound with twine and resemble shut-tight umbrellas. I can only imagine how piney-good that truck smells. We don't carry live Christmas trees, which is why Grampa Chris never minded the charity tree lot across the street. Actually, I think he liked it. He liked the library and he liked seeing all the families out choosing their just-right tree and strapping it to the roof of their car. He liked that most of those families dropped by our shop later for strings of lights and ornaments too.

I watch Hector lift whole trees out of the truck and toss them effortlessly into a neat stack at the edge of the lot. And then stop and look over and see me watching. Dang. Why am I watching?

He lifts a gloved hand and waves. I wave back. After a couple more tree tosses, Hector smacks the arm of another Bunyan and points across Fair Street at me. The other guy nods and Hector walks off the lot and toward the road.

The afternoon traffic on Fair Street comes in clumps, broken up by stoplights on the nearby corner of Main to the west and the more distant Hill Street, about a half mile to the east. Hector jogs toward the southbound lane.

I wave again, but then feel stupid standing there waiting for him. I point to the path he can take around the North Pole to the staff breakroom, then duck in through the front door as quietly as I can. I'd rather not have Bryan and Aunt Carole know that I'm here, even though it is my afternoon off and I shouldn't be expected to be working.

Still, Dad told me last night that they are watching my Productivity. Carole thinks I might be chatting too much at the desk and slowing things down. She suspects I might not be being Efficient. Dad tells me that he told her he knows I'm doing my best.

Before I started writing Santa letters, the phrase *doing her best* would have cheered me, but since I have written some variation of that statement more than one hundred times and know it for the reassuring but utterly empty statement that it is, I'm not so flattered.

"I *am* doing my best," I told him anyway. "There are only a couple dozen letters to go." I don't tell him about Alice helping me out on Sunday just in case he feels impressed enough with my progress to tell Aunt Carole and to demand a Pillar Point or two on my behalf.

The breakroom is empty. I pace. I pick a mug up from the drying rack. "Elves Are People Too," it says. I consider tossing the mug in the trash but put it in the cupboard instead. "Would you like a cookie?" I say out loud. It sounds okay. Normal. I take out a plate to put the cookies on. Then I put the plate back. Then the door opens. Thanks to the parking lot sound system, I can hear Bing Crosby duetting "White Christmas" with that woman nobody knows the name of. And then Hector is in the breakroom.

"Nice shirt," I tell him. I practiced saying that too.

"My brother bought them for the whole tree crew. He calls us LumberJuans."

"Brilliant."

"It'd be brilliant if he hadn't copied it from *Lumberjanes.* You know that comic?"

I don't.

"Oh," says Hector. "It's good. You should read it."

He adjusts his hat.

I adjust my hair.

He adjusts his hat again.

"Would you like a cookie?" I ask. "My gram made them."

"Sure," says Hector. "Thanks."

I decapitate the snowman, pull out a few cookies, and set them on an "Only for the Big Guy" plate.

"I'm the Big Guy?" asks Hector.

If Sam Spinek had said this I would know that he was being disgusting, but Hector doesn't seem disgusting. Although it seems like he has just realized that I might interpret him that way. A blush darkens his cheeks, complimenting the cardinal of his plaid.

"So this is where you work?" he asks.

"Mostly I work at the shop." I point a cookie across the parking lot. "Except for when we have Santa School or there's some office work to do."

"Santa School?" asks Hector. "There's a school for Santas? What do they do? Santa math? Santa geography?"

"Actually, they do both," I tell him. It's true. "Some Santas do charity work exclusively and donate their time, but most are small businessmen—or women; we teach

Ms. Santas too." I don't bring up the elves. "They charge fees and do taxes and buy insurance. Santa math is a real thing."

"And geography?" says Hector.

"Okay, so you're some kid visiting Indiana from, say, Ecuador, and you show up at the mall and you go sit on Santa's lap and you tell him that you are from Ecuador, right? Santa knows everything. EVERYTHING. So he knows where Ecuador is and he knows what the weather is like and he can't ask stupid questions like, 'Is that in Ohio?' or 'Should I bring you a sled for Christmas?'"

"And these Santas learn that from you?"

"From my dad. Before him, they learned it from my Grampa Chris. He was the real-deal Santa. He loved it. Loved Christmas. And he was absolutely disgusted by screw-up Santas. He'd see guys in hotel lobbies and at children's parties wearing sloppy suits and cheap beards with the elastic showing and doing stupid things like flirting with moms or calling kids by the wrong name. It made my grampa nuts. He had heard about Santa schools in other places, but there wasn't one nearby and he knew a lot of the local guys wouldn't pay a lot of money to go to schools out of state, so he started a school here."

Hector is smiling at this. At me.

"Do you think it's funny?" I ask him.

"No," he says. "Not at all. I just wish I could see it."

"Well, you can see where we do the classes." Hector and I stand up and I take a step toward Snowflake, then stop. Snowflake would be quiet. Dark. We'd be all alone without the risk of cookie-seeking employees busting in for their break. All at once, I feel half naked. Like I'm in my swimsuit.

"Actually," I say, "I forgot. There's stuff spread out all over in there."

"Oh," says Hector. "Okay. Well, maybe I could see where you keep all the decorated trees? One of our customers at the lot said it was beautiful."

The Tree Shed? Even worse. Hector must read something in my face because he's already retracting his request. "Never mind," he says. "I mean, I get it. You're on your break. No big deal."

It feels like a big deal. It feels like a very big deal. And like Hector senses that I've closed a door on something. "I, um. I could show you something else. I could—oh, I could show you the letters!"

I give him another cookie and dash off to Snowflake. When I return, I set the box of yet-to-be-answered letters on the breakroom table. "I don't know if you are aware," I say to him, "but I am known to the children of Hollydale as Santa's Intern."

"No kidding," says Hector.

"It was on cable access television, so you know it is true. *An Evening with Santa.* Except Santa couldn't make it so I subbed in. I have a serious following."

"I can see that." Hector plucks an envelope from the box and looks at the address. "'Santa's Innards,'" he reads.

"Sad state of modern education," I say. "Today's six-year-olds have not been taught about the capitalist innovation of unpaid labor in the name of 'getting experience.' They've never heard the word *intern* before, so they write down whatever they think they heard."

"In whatever spelling they can, it looks like." Hector pulls a few more envelopes from the bin. "'Santa's Inturn . . . Santa's Entirn.' These three got it right . . . 'Santa's'—oh, now that's—" He's laughing. He's trying not to, I can tell, but he's laughing. He pushes the envelope across the table.

Santa's Inturd.

I can't help it. I laugh too. "No way that kid is getting a pony for Christmas," I say.

"Do you see a lot of pony requests?"

"Not really. One so far. Mostly kids want electronics. Some action figures. Video games are big."

"Puppies. The best kids want puppies." Alice drops her schoolbag on the table, then turns her back to Hector so she can make just-between-the-two-of-us-holy-smokes-this-boy-is-cute eyebrows at me.

"I didn't hear you come in," I say.

"My ninja training is paying off. Plus there was a lot of loud laughing going on in here. I'm Alice," she says to Hector. "Intern to Santa's Intern . . . wait." Her eyes catch the envelope in front of me and a look of absolute glee passes over her. "Does this really and truly say *Inturd*?"

I nod.

"Mine!" she yells, scooping it off the table.

"Hey! You don't even know if there's a puppy plea in it."

"I don't care. *Inturd* is mine. Oh, kid." She flips the envelope over for the return address. "Oh, Jordan Swan of 1224 Sparrow Ridge Road, you have made my day." She flops into a chair and pats the envelope happily. "Are you here to help?" she asks Hector. "Do not despair that you have lost out on being the Inturd. I'm sure there are some other good ones in there. Francie was an Internist once."

"You went to medical school?" says Hector.

"Online course," I say. "I'm really a podiatrist. The kid was confused."

Alice grins and turns to Hector. "Sit down, um, what's your name? Sam, right?"

Hector's smile dips, just for a second. "Hector. And I can't stay. I'm sorry, Francie. Maybe I can help with the letters some other time, but my brother is waiting for me at the lot." He sets his cookie plate by the sink.

"We didn't talk about the homework," I say.

"It's okay. I'll figure it out. Thanks for the cookies."

I nod and he's gone.

Alice waits until the breakroom door closes. "Hector," she says.

"Hector," I say.

"Not Sam."

"Not Sam."

She attempts an eyebrow apology.

"You're not advanced enough," I say.

"Sorry about that." I'm not sure whether she is apologizing about the boy mix-up or about her eyebrow inferiority, but it doesn't matter. It's not like Hector showed a single sign of liking me. And even if he did? Then what?

"You didn't do anything," I tell her. "It doesn't matter. It's . . . do you want to do some letters? We might even be able to finish this today."

We take the box of letters back into Snowflake.

"'Dear Jordan,'" says Alice as she writes.

I pull a letter from the bin and do the same. "'Dear Otis.'"

27

Aunt Carole's response to the complaints about her wreath runs in this week's edition of the *Hollydale Daily*. It includes the words *unsophisticated, stuck in the past,* and *wouldn't know good taste if it crashed into her Dodge Durango.* Claims are also made about the sorts of wreaths one sees in chic European towns like Paris, Amsterdam, and . . . Frankfurter. It was this last bit that the editor of the *Hollydale Daily* had called Aunt Carole about, but before he could get to any specifics she threatened to pull all of the Holiday Shop's advertising. Thus, Frankfurter.

"Frankfurter," says my dad at dinner. Mom is at the shop and Dad has come home to eat with Gram, me, and the twins. Gram has not read the paper yet.

"It's kielbasa, dear," she tells him. "I probably should

have made sauerkraut to go with it, but Don and Dash wanted mac and cheese."

"It's delicious. Thanks, Mom."

Gram waves away her thanks. "If I weren't here with the boys in the afternoon and making dinner for you all, I'd just be rattling around alone in my apartment," she says.

"We like you rattling around here," says Dash. It's a rare sweet moment from my brother. He knows that Gram has made brownies for dessert.

"How's school, Francie?" asks Gram.

"It's okay," I tell her.

"Boys keep sticking out their tongues at her," says Don.

I choke on my mac and cheese.

"Oh, they are not," says Gram. "Francie is in high school, Donner. High school boys don't behave like that."

"Where'd you hear that?" I ask Don.

"Hockey," says Dash. "Gordie Hobbes told us."

My brothers do peewee hockey. Of course there are younger puckheads among their ranks.

"Well, Gordie Hobbes is mistaken," says Gram. "Right, Nick?"

My dad startles at his name. "What? Sorry, Mom. I was just thinking about the tr—"

He sounds like he's about to say "Tree Shed" but then he looks at me and says "transfers" instead. "The transfers I need to take care of. Employee stuff. Moving new people from one department to another."

It sounds plausible, but in the fifteen years I've been around that store, I've never heard of anything called a transfer of employees. I don't think Gram has either, but she plays along. "The transfers," she says. "Well, you have a lot on your mind, I know. I wish you'd take a break more often, though. You look tired."

Dad does look tired. Exhausted, really. But I can tell that he would like the topic to change from his being tired as much as I wanted it to when Don was speaking of tongues. As soon as Dad can he excuses himself from the table and goes back to the shop. I do the dishes, then follow Dad's lead, excusing myself to go to my bedroom. "I have homework," I tell Gram, "but I'll keep my door open so I can hear Don and Dash. You can go home if you want."

"Yeah," says Dash. "You can go home. We'll be good for Francie." The boys flank Gram, encircling her waist with twin-action hugs.

"Such thoughtful children," she says, rubbing their backs. Easy for her to say. She can't see their faces. They are looking at me, eyes crossed, tongues stuck out as far as they will go.

28

On the breakroom table is a copy of the most recent *Hollydale Daily*. Someone has left it open to the editorial page on which there is another short complaint about the disco wreath. The words *newfangled* and *flashy* and the phrase *Vanity versus public security* are used. Just below it is an editorial cartoon featuring a holiday wreath made entirely of sparkly silver hot dogs. "Christmas in Frankfurter," it says in the caption.

I can't wait to show Alice.

Before she gets here, I check my in-box and find a note. Bryan's rigid printing informs me that the local cable station rebroadcasted *An Evening with Santa* on Monday after the school board failed to reach a quorum and spontaneously canceled its regularly scheduled live cable access televised meeting.

As a result, there are more letters waiting for me in Snowflake.

Also it appears that a few of the regional newspapers have picked up the *Hollydale Daily* story (about Santa's Intern, not the disco wreath). Those stories, most of which exist on web versions of their papers, have embedded a clip from the cable broadcast in which I instruct a tearful Jessilyn to write to me to make sure Santa gets her message. Thus, there are now three new boxes of letters in Snowflake.

I can't help but think of Sisyphus, condemned by Zeus to shove a massive boulder up the side of a mountain only to have it roll back down at the end of every day. Ms. Colando called Sisyphus the trickster king of Corinth and said that twice he had actually outsmarted Zeus, but the third time Zeus got him. I can't help but wonder if between attempts two and three Zeus hired himself an intern.

Twenty-two days. Just twenty-two good days and I'll get my raise. Miata, I remind myself. Sunshine-yellow autonomy. Top-down driving, me and Alice having the freedom to sing as loud as we want and go where we want, when we want.

> *Dear Veeda:*
>   *Santa thinks black hair is just as beautiful*
>   *as blond, maybe more (don't tell).*

Dear Wyatt:

Santa loves soccer but thinks you should only play if you want to.

Dear Alyssa:

Santa thanks you for the suggestion about the mints. He is sorry that the helper Santa you met at the mall had onions for lunch.

The door to Snowflake opens and Alice pokes her head inside. "Look what I found." She angles a tray through the doorway. On it is a stack of cookies and three coffee cups.

"Darling cookie angel!" I say, and I'm about to ask if the third cup is because she has telepathically intuited how tired I am when a fine-shouldered LumberJuan follows her into the room.

"He was pacing in the parking lot."

"I wasn't pacing." A blush floods Hector's cheeks. "I have a Fitbit." He lifts a sleeve for proof. "My cousin is a fitness instructor. She's counting my steps on hockey days versus nonhockey days. It's for a study. She . . . I . . ." He drops his sleeve. "I wasn't pacing," he says again.

Alice sets the tray on the long worktable. She's got a smirk on her face like Gram's cat, Bumble, wears when he's brought her a particularly gory mouse. "Have a cookie and grab a pen," she tells Hector.

I shoot Alice a what-are-you-doing look, which she must mistake for a please-meddle-in-this-and-make-it-as-uncomfortable-as-possible look. She steers Hector into the seat beside me. "Sit there, next to Francie. She'll show you what to do."

Hector sits. Alice grins.

"Closer," she says. "So Francie can watch you work." She lifts her eyebrows lasciviously. *Curse you, Miss Fisher!*

"You don't have to," I say. I'd shoot Alice a stop-it look, but she'd probably book us a wedding planner.

"Are you kidding? Look at all these letters." Alice makes her voice like the lady on the Catholic Charities commercial. "We need your help."

Hector looks at the boxes.

"Think of the children," she continues.

Hector must think of the children because he pulls out his phone and does some quick, not-messed-up texting. "Okay. My brother doesn't need me at the tree lot until five. How can I help?"

Alice nudges his chair even closer to mine, hands Hector a letter, and retreats to her side of the table.

Hector studies the letter. I read over his significant shoulder. It is a very pleasant way to read.

"So," Hector says. "Alex wants a Fairy Ninja Twin doll and she—or they or he, maybe—loves the Pacers," says Hector.

"Impressive," says Alice.

It is impressive. Right away, Hector realizes that Alex could be a name for anyone. Also, he is a master decoder. Alex's letter has some of the most creative spelling I've seen, but Hector doesn't stumble and knows instantly that P-A-S-U-R-E-S refers to Indiana's pro basketball team.

"Very impressive," I agree.

"So, what do I do?" asks Hector.

"Mention the Pacers in your reply and the doll, too, just in case Alex's parents didn't see the letter before it got sent. Don't say Santa will bring the doll or try to bring the doll or anything like that."

"No?" asks Hector.

"'Santa will do his best to make your Christmas special,'" I tell him.

"Okay," he says. "Got it."

I watch him write. I keep my hands at my sides and try to look at something other than his shoulders. For example, Hector has a neck. And right at his hairline, just below his right ear, are six tiny freckles, just a little darker than his skin. If you connected them, I think, they would look like the Big Dipper. Or the Little Dipper. Some-size darling, adorable Dipper.

"Do I have crumbs? Did I—" Hector brushes away the cookie crumbs he imagines I've been staring at.

"You're fine," I say.

Alice snorts.

We all write together for a while, the silence broken only when Hector needs advice, Alice needs more cookies, or someone gets a letter with an unusual request.

"This one wants to open a restaurant and needs a wood-fired pizza oven," says Alice.

"Ambitious," says Hector.

"A great many of our correspondents are entrepreneurial," I tell him. "A couple of days ago an aspiring zookeeper wrote seeking a baby elephant and any spare reindeer Santa might have around the place."

Hector riffles through his letters. "I have one. . . . Here it is: 'Dear Santa, I have been very good. I like gym. I do not like science class. For Christmas, I would like no more science class.'"

"Poor kid. Santa is powerful but even he can't fight state curriculum standards," says Alice.

I open a new letter and scan the page. "Ha!" I say. "This kid wants her mom to make more money."

"Me too, Intern," says Alice. "Get on that."

I skim the letter and read aloud. "'I would like a book called *Charlotte's Web* because I got one from Elf Shelly but the end was missing.'" Elf Shelly. I picture some jingle-belled show-off cartwheeling around a shopping center parking lot hurling defective books at fearful children. "Elves," I mutter.

Alice laughs.

Hector slips the letter from my hand and reads it. "Not Elf Shelly. Elf Shelf. It's a pop-up food pantry. There was one in Gary last Christmas. There's probably one in Hollydale too." He reads the whole letter aloud.

> *Dear Santa's Intern:*
> *I saw you on TV at my aunt's house. You*

said you can tell Santa things. Please tell
him for Christmas my mom wants a job that
makes more money. If he can do it, please
tell him I would like a book for Christmas.
I would like a book called Charlotte's Web
because I got one from Elf Shelf but the end
was missing. If he can't bring the book,
could Santa just tell me what happens? He
could put a note in my stocking. I will be at
my aunt's house probably.
    Your friend,
    Olivia

"Well," says Alice after a minute. "That is a lot less funny."

Hector turns to me. "Does Santa's Intern ever just send a gift? Could we just mail this kid a copy of the book?"

I start to tell him we'd have to contact Olivia's mom first but Hector's already reaching for the envelope. "There's no return address," he says.

Most of the time when there's no return address, I'm relieved—one less letter to write.

But not this time.

"Give me that," says Alice.

Hector slides Olivia's letter across the table. Alice reads and a grin spreads across her face.

"This is it," she says.

"You found an address?"

Alice waves the letter. "This is my story. The one that gets me in the *Daily*. I'm going to track down Olivia, and you, Santa's Intern, are going to give her the book she wants for Christmas," she says. "Front-page story. Photo. The works." In less than a minute, Alice is on the phone with somebody at the Hollydale Food Pantry, which runs the Elf Shelf pop-ups. Alice asks a lot of questions and says a lot of *uh-huh*s and *that's true*s and *okay*s and finally ends the call saying "See you then" and texting herself a bunch of notes.

"Did you find her?" I ask.

Alice shakes her head and keeps texting. "The person I talked to didn't know any Olivias, but she says there are a lot of volunteers who also work at the pantry and I can come down there tomorrow after school and talk to people if I want."

"That sounds good." Hector pulls a ten out of his wallet and hands it to Alice. "Do you think you'll have a chance to buy a copy of the book before you go? Just in case someone knows her? You could ask them to pass it along?"

"Wait a second," I say. I've been to a lot of Santa Schools. I've heard Santas tell stories about charity events where each kid gets something off their list, but this feels different. I mean, we aren't the Rotary Club or a neighborhood community center. We're just three teenagers in a seasonally themed conference room.

"What?" asks Hector. "Is something wrong?" He's looking at me. I can't see the Dipper, but I know it is there. Nothing is wrong. How could anything be wrong? "Francie?"

"Um, it doesn't feel right, you paying for this. I'm the Intern." I find a five and four ones at the bottom of my backpack. I've been depositing my entire biweekly paycheck into my bank account and taking out only the barest minimum, so this is all the cash I have. Alice takes it.

"You can both pay," she says. "The kid deserves a hardcover."

Her phone vibrates then. "Dad," she says. "He's on his way to pick me up. Hey, didn't you say you had to be at the tree lot at five?" She flashes Hector her phone. It is 4:52.

Hector leaps from his seat. "I gotta go," he says. "Thanks for letting me be an intern to the Intern," he says, and he's out the door.

There's barely enough time for Alice to offer another lascivious eyebrow before he returns. "I really wasn't pacing," he says to me.

"Fitbit," I agree.

"But I was thinking—I was going to ask—Do you . . . do you guys, I mean, do both of you, ever go to the Torino on Thursdays?"

The Torino is this club at the edge of Hollydale which, on Thursday nights, hosts an alcohol-free night for teens. There's a DJ and sometimes a couple of performances by high school bands and comedians and artists, but mostly, I have heard, there is dancing and a lot of making out, which is why I haven't gone. Not the dancing. I like dancing. The other part.

"No," I say at the exact same time that Alice says, "Why?"

"I was thinking of going this Thursday and just wondered if you, you guys, if both of you, would be there."

I don't say anything. The boy has constellation skin. Would we be there? Why wouldn't we be there?

"Francie has to work on Thursdays," says Alice.

Oh yeah. That is why.

"I can ask for a Thursday off." I try not to sound too excited and end up sounding more like robotic Bryan than I'd like. "Not this pay period, but next maybe?" I count the days on my fingers. "So, the fifteenth? I could ask."

Hector looks at his Fitbit like it's a watch. "Good. Okay. I just wanted to know. I was wondering."

Alice flashes her phone at him again and he's gone.

"He likes you," sings Alice. "He just asked you out."

"He didn't," I tell her. "He asked us both out. Or asked if we were going to be out. To be at the Torino."

Alice lifts an eyebrow in that best-friend-in-the-movies-who-knows-things way. This time I'd like her to be right.

29

As soon as we're in our Mythology Today discussion groups, Hector leans toward me. He smells like pine trees. I know that's a trope about boys in books, but in this case, probably because of the Christmas tree lot, it is also accurate. *In a world where the night sky sleeps behind the ear of a pine-scented boy . . .*

"Was Alice able to get the book to that kid?" he asks.

Book? Book, yes. "Yes," I tell him. "I mean, she was able to get a copy of the book, but none of the Elf Shelf volunteers knew any girl named Olivia, so Alice left it in the Little Free Library there."

"Oh." Hector stops leaning.

"Do you want your ten dollars back?" I ask. Not that I have cash to give him right now.

"That's okay," says Hector. "Alice did the right thing. Olivia might find it there."

"She might," I tell him. But then I tell him the other things that Alice learned, like that there are actually two Elf Shelfs within a thirty-mile radius, both of which are in the broadcast zone of Hollydale Cable. Olivia might have gone to either of them.

"I could donate another twenty dollars, I guess. Although it would be good to have at least two copies in each library, right? In case one gets checked out?"

"That's sixty," says DeKieser, who has been listening.

"Sixty what?" asks Ellie, who has not.

Hector explains. She looks bored until she hears about me being Santa's Intern. "Wait," she says to me. "You dress up every day?"

"Not every day. Just for work," I tell her.

"You dress up and you write letters and do little elf things?"

"No. No elf things. I'm not—"

Ms. Colando tugs at her Mystery Shack Staff shirt and reminds us that we should be talking in classroom voices.

"Too bad you can't, like, just give every family at the place a book or whatever."

I sneak my phone out of my backpack and pull up the texts Alice sent me with her article research. "Each location serves about two hundred households and"—I scroll down—"about half of them have kids under twelve."

"And each book is, like, twenty dollars?" asks DeKieser.

I check online. "Nine in paper," I tell her.

"That's, like, retail or whatever. My mom's a teacher. She sometimes gets, like, half-off bulk books for school sales and stuff. If we could get that or whatever . . ." DeKieser scribbles in her notebook. "About nine hundred."

"Nine hundred what?" says Ellie.

"Dollars. To buy a book for each family."

Hector slumps in his chair. "If it wasn't Christmas, I *might* be able to do ninety dollars, but nine hundred?"

I slump too. Nine hundred dollars is a lot of money. Almost a quarter of an uncle-discounted Miata.

Ellie shrugs. "I have to see a man . . ." She begs a bathroom pass from Ms. Colando and heads for the halls.

"I guess we should, like, discuss mythology or whatever," says DeKieser.

We discuss mythology. DeKieser talks about college application questions.

Hector tells me to go next and I'm halfway through explaining how the first Christmas parade was really just an advertisement for a New York department store when Ellie comes back into the room.

"It's done," she says, sliding into her seat and pushing up her glasses.

"What's done?" asks Hector.

"The deal. Listen, I've got a slot at the Torino in two weeks. I was going to show this film I did about the manhole covers of Indiana, but it's a bit subtle for the teen minds of Hollydale," she tells him. "So instead, I'm going to debut a new short film—about her."

She is looking at me. Why is she looking at me?

"*The Secret Life of Santa's Intern*," she says.

"I don't think so," I say. *An Evening with Santa* was enough screen time for me. And while I am currently a celebrity among the under-nine set, most of Hollydale High School seems ignorant of my indignity. No way am I going to broaden my humiliation to the PG-13 crowd.

"And you will do the voice-overs and the interviewing," she says to Hector.

"I already told you, E. I don't have time for your—"

"And you are promotion and finances," she tells DeKieser, who is the only one of us who seems happy with this announcement.

"What am I promoting? Like, the show or the film or—?" she asks.

"Nothing," I tell her. "There's not going to be a film."

Ellie ignores me. "I just got off the phone with Bruce at the Torino. They're willing to donate half of the admission to a book drive as long as we run a food drive too. You'd only need to get about a hundred and fifty people there."

"A hundred and seventy," says DeKieser.

Hector leans again, this time toward Ellie. "Really?" he asks.

"Really," says Ellie. "But Bruce will only do this for me, his beloved niece. It could raise the money you need. But unless I have a film to screen . . . " She trails off deliberately, then shrugs.

"You'll have a film," says Hector. "I mean, if Francie wants . . ."

Ellie looks at me. *No,* I think. *No way.* Hector bumps his shoulder against mine. Did I already mention what fine shoulders he has?

"You'll have a film," I say.

30

Several times over the next week, Ellie and Hector ride my bus home with me or beg a ride to the shop from a sibling or friend. Alice meets us when she can, which isn't often, since she's working on her big story for the *Daily*. They've given her the go-ahead to write about the event at the Torino on Thursday and to cover the delivery of books and donated goods to the Elf Shelf on Saturday afternoon. In the meantime, she's doing background research about food pantries and hungry families, so when she is here with us, she's not exactly jolly.

Ellie, however, is thrilled. At school she can be sort of cool and detached, but behind her camera she's all joy. It matters to her, this film. She shoots and reshoots. She tells Hector to move props and ask questions. She hides when Bryan or Aunt Carole are around.

Whether I am at the Intern Desk or in Snowflake, I do what I always do. I respond to Intern letters.

> *Dear Willa:*
> *I will remind Santa about your love of NASCAR.*

> *Dear Kiddo:*
> *Your parents can have a fire in the fireplace. Santa doesn't mind using the front door.*

> *Dear Charys:*
> *Santa loves treats, but you can tell your friend Lacie that the number of cookies you leave him has nothing to do with how many gifts he'll put in your stocking.*

"That's good to know," says Hector.

This afternoon, I'm at my Santa's Intern desk on the salesfloor while Ellie is outside getting footage of the entrance and some of the other buildings. She wanted some shots of the sleigh Dad drove in the Hollydale Holiday Parade on Sunday, but I told her that unless Uncle Jack was in there getting Rudolph ready for his maintenance in Peoria, the door to the garage would probably be locked. And if he was in there, she still had better stay clear. It is likely that my family will find out about Ellie's film project at some point, but they don't need to know how much of it was shot here while I was supposed to be earning Pillar Points with my dedication to Intern duty. Right now, my dad believes that I'm spending every spare minute writing Intern letters—even when I'm not on the clock—and I can't help enjoying the pride in his eyes. It reminds me of the way that Grampa Chris used to look at Dad when he stepped up to give Santa School lectures or developed the new inventory system for the shop.

"You sure I can't help you with those?" says Hector. "If you give me a pen, I could move aside a couple of these outdoor light sets and work right here."

"Now how would that look to the children?" I say. Truth is, it is not the children I'm thinking about. It's not like we're tucked away in Snowflake. We're right here in the middle of this customer-filled shop. If my dad did walk by and see anyone but me writing these letters I'm certain that his look of pride would be replaced by a fairly angry one. Best, I think, to let him believe his faith in me is warranted.

I hear sleigh bells at the front of the store and a moment later Ellie is at the desk. "I took a couple of shots through the garage window. You were right. Your uncle was in there. I got some footage of him moving some reindeer around." She looks at her phone. "I only have a few minutes left before my mom picks me up. Can we get in that tree building now?"

Ellie wants to film the Tree Shed. Who can blame her?

It's probably the most magical part of the whole shop. She's got this idea that her movie will start sort of kitschy but at the end there will be some serious heartstring pulling. For a while she kept directing me to tell her something deep and meaningful about Christmas or Santa, but every time I tried she would motion for me to get teary-eyed, which only made me laugh. After five or six attempts, she finally gave up. "I'll fix it in editing," she told me, but I can't help but feel her camera always at the ready, just in case I spontaneously weep.

I put my SANTA'S INTERN WILL RETURN SOON sign on the desk and tell Dottie I'm going to grab my jacket from the coat closet and go outside for my break. She looks at Hector, then winks at me. "Enjoy," she says.

"Dottie!" I say under my breath. "There's nothing going on."

"Have faith," she says.

It is freezing outside and I hug my coat tight around me. The sky is gray, the trees are leafless. There is still no snow. "Let nothing you dismay," Mahalia Jackson sings to the cars in the parking lot. "I'm doing the best I can" is what I want to tell Mahalia.

We make our way to the Tree Shed, with Ellie chattering about how the film is mostly edited and how it's going to be fantastic and how it is too bad she's screening during the DJ break at the Torino alcohol-free teen night and not at a proper film festival, but at least there will be an audience.

"You really think people will come?" I'll admit, I'm

more concerned about this on my own behalf than I am on Ellie's. To get all those copies of *Charlotte's Web* to the Elf Shelf by this Saturday, DeKieser's mom had to order them right away, and to secure the discount, they needed to be paid for in advance. Since the only one of us with enough money in the bank to make such a payment was me, there is now a nine-hundred-dollar hole in my Miata fund. I have been assured by DeKieser and everyone else that the hole will be filled. That people will come. That DeKieser's marketing campaign is a good one. Of that last claim, I have proof. There is not a hallway, not a bulletin board, not a bathroom stall in all of Hollydale High School that does not have one of DeKieser's flyers taped to it. They are good flyers, too. All the details are spelled out: the date, the time, the admission fee, the food donations, the very good cause. (And not a *like, stuff,* or *whatever* anywhere, by the way.) Those details are not what makes the flyer so persuasive, however. It is the big, bold print at the bottom of the flyer: THERE WILL BE MISTLETOE.

When we reach the Tree Shed I wave to the two employees inside and one of them comes out to meet me. I tell the employee, Deanna, that Ellie is going to take some footage of the trees and not to worry about her.

"Okay," says Ellie. "Let's get started." She props open the huge glass doors at the entrance and walks backward into the Tree Shed, camera turned on me. "Take off your coat and come with me," she says.

I don't move. "I'm going to stay out here," I say.

"What? Why? I need you in here, marveling at the magic of the holiday. Eyes full of wonder. Tears of joy, maybe?"

My throat tightens and for the first time since we started filming I'm pretty sure I could manage some tears, but I'm determined not to. "I can't go in," I tell Ellie, because that is the truth. "I have to stay here and be on lookout. If my dad or my aunt or Bryan came by while we were filming, I'd be in trouble." Which is also the truth, though it is not the reason I can't go in.

"Fine," says Ellie. "Fine . . . just take off your coat, okay?" She takes my coat from me and tosses it behind one of the doors. "Hector," she says, "can *you* step over the threshold, at least? I need someone to tell me if I'm going to bump into something." Hector gives me a quick look, then takes his place behind Ellie, who continues walking backward, keeping her camera fixed on me. I imagine what it looks like on her screen, the shot widening to take in more Christmas magic with every step, and me standing outside shivering, shrinking smaller and smaller in the frame.

I look pathetic. I'm sure I do. But I haven't been in the Tree Shed for two Christmases now—not when my dad asked me to help him decorate the Frozen Fir, not when Uncle Jack promised to hold my hand, not when this year's Santa students did their memorial.

The last time I was in the Tree Shed, I wasn't supposed to be.

It was summer, just two weeks after I had learned what a failure I had been at all things kissing related. The neighborhood boys were still teasing me then and I had spied one of them in the store parking lot with his mom. Chances were he wouldn't bother me in her presence, but just in case I looked around for a place to hide and noticed that the tree lights were on in the shed.

When you grow up in a family like mine there are things that you know better than most people, like all those colors of red, and the history of elves, and the origins of Christmas parades. You also know better than most how expensive it is to run lights for twenty-four Christmas trees, and so seeing those lights on and finding the door to the shed unlocked felt sort of like a Christmas-in-August miracle. Who was I to turn down a miracle? I said a quick thank-you to the universe and ducked inside.

At first I didn't even notice him. I was still looking at the tree lights. The Gumdrop Express train was running too. And the automatons—Mrs. Claus blowing out her candle, Santa checking his list. That elf.

And then, there he was. Grampa Chris, facedown on the path. There was a lot of blood.

The blood was dark. Burgundy. Mahogany.

At first I thought it was a bloody nose. I mean, it was a bloody nose—but that wasn't all it was. The paramedics said the bloody nose happened when he fell.

He fell because he had a heart attack about a half hour before I got there.

I must have used my phone to call Dad because a minute later he was there. And then my mom was there. And then Gram.

Gram went still when she saw Grampa Chris. Dad did, too, after that. And Mom.

Everything was still except the train and the Clauses and the elf only a few feet away from Grampa Chris's outstretched arm, that elf deciding over and over again that the present he'd taken from the pack wasn't one he wanted to give after all.

Later, Gram had questions. What was he doing in here? Was he checking inventory? Was he putting out stock? What was he doing in here all alone? Had he been feeling bad and come into the shed to cheer himself up?

Bloodstains are a blackish-brownish red that I don't know any other name for. If the stains are small it can sometimes take a while to notice them. There were some, I heard, in the Faux Snow right in front of the elf. Nobody noticed until November, when the Tree Shed was opened for the season. If it had been real snow, the stains would have soaked in or melted away, but since it wasn't real, Jerry from Receiving cut the stained piece out and patched it with new stuff, which at first was too white but after a while wasn't.

You can't tell the difference now, I've been told.

I could go check for myself, I guess.

There are some things you could know better than most people, but you choose not to.

31

DECEMBER 15

The plan is this: The Torino opens at eight o'clock. Hector and his older brother, Luis, will pick Alice and me up at the North Pole twenty minutes earlier and drive us there. Alice's dad, who is not sure he trusts a boy to bring his daughter home so late, will pick us girls up at the end of the evening when Luis comes back for Hector.

Alice and I answer a bunch of Intern letters and then she changes into her Torino wear: a burgundy velvet blazer, fishnet tights, and the black skirt I was supposed to have worn last month instead of the pea-green, candy-caned mortification that started this whole uniform mess. Alice forgot to bring shoes, but her Regina, Queen of Heaven saddle shoes give her outfit just the right quirky edge. It has been decided that for press purposes, I must wear my Corporate Christmas uniform.

"You look fine," says Alice. "Adorable. I like how you matched your lipstick to your tie."

"Thank you," I say.

"And do not underestimate how cute your butt looks in those elf shorts."

"*Elf* shorts? Not you too."

Alice squinches her eyebrows in a way that is either an apology or a mockery of one.

Just then Hector knocks on the breakroom door. "Ready?" he says. He's got a leather jacket on over a maroon V-neck sweater and black jeans. The jeans fit very well. I can say this objectively, but when I tell him he looks nice, it sounds anything but objective. Alice eyebrows me again. This time there's no confusion. She thinks his jeans fit well too.

There is a line outside the Torino when we arrive, but Ellie is waiting for us and drags us inside to where DeKieser is standing, flanked by a pretty blond girl and surrounded by canned goods. Beyond her, I can see into the whole of the Torino. The dance floor is already crowded. "This is so great!" shouts Alice over the thumping bass.

"Actually, it's, like, only kind of great," says DeKieser. She introduces us to the blond girl, Kelsey, who is her date for the evening, then sends Kelsey off to get sodas while she explains the situation to us. Apparently, despite the clarity of DeKieser's flyers, the guy letting people into the

Torino was under the impression that in order to enjoy a night of alcohol-free underage fun, Torino-goers must surrender *either* the ten-dollar admission fee *or* make a food donation. I look at the tower of canned beets.

"So none of these people paid admission?" I ask.

"It's been totally corrected now or whatever. Like, everyone else will pay. But, um, yeah."

I do the Miata math. There must be a hundred people in there. At 50% of ten dollars each . . . that's five hundred dollars. Five hundred dollars that should have gone back into my Miata fund.

Ellie pulls on one of her curls. "You're just going to have to make a really good speech," she says.

Wait. "What speech?" I don't know anything about a speech.

Ellie hands me a schedule for the night's alcohol-free, teen-centric events. Right now is dancing. In an hour, something called the Lloyd Dobler Octet will do a fifteen-minute set. Then Ellie will show her film, which will be followed by a few words from Santa's Intern herself. Finally, when everyone is thoroughly bored, dancing will resume until the lights go back on at eleven and the lot of us are kicked out.

"Just, like, say how you're glad people came and whatever and tell them stuff about the food pantry and the book and, like, whatever. And how they can donate more and—"

"And stuff. Yeah. Thanks." I instantly feel awful for

mocking DeKieser, but she gives me a pass, most likely attributing my rudeness to nerves.

Ellie thinks I am nervous too. "You'll be fine," she says, though she's not very reassuring, actually. This is mostly because she is not giving it much effort. She is surveying the room. I watch her watch. There are people on the dance floor and at the alcohol-free bar, and clustering at the tables. But what Ellie is watching is a ten-foot space between the bar and the tables, a space which, I assume, will be full of dancers once all the people in line are actually inside, but right now has only a trio of boys, oddly spaced.

I watch a girl—a junior, one of Mina's friends if I remember right—try to keep the two sodas she's carrying from sloshing over their rims as she zigzags around the boys at top speed. This does not keep at least two of the boys from grinning expectantly at her.

"What's going on?" I ask.

Ellie lifts her chin toward the ceiling. It is difficult to see in the dim light but dangling above the heads of each of the boys is a baseball-size wad of leaves and berries.

"Mistletoe minefield," says Ellie.

"You're kidding," I say.

She isn't. "My uncle says the weekend singles love it."

We watch another girl dart into the field, though she slows down significantly in front of a boy in a plaid scarf. A kiss on the cheek results. The girl returns the gesture and looks pleased about it. "I guess I know one spot I'll be avoiding tonight," I say nonetheless.

"Better hope you don't have to pee, then." Ellie points to the glowing restroom sign just beyond the minefield.

I set down my soda. "Thanks for the warning."

The Torino is filling up. Many of the people here look familiar, but they aren't all from Hollydale. Some are Regina girls and I recognize a few boys from my days at Our Lady of Sorrows. Out on the dance floor, Alice dances with DeKieser and Kelsey and one of the undisciplined Lutherans from her party bus.

"She looks like she's having fun," says Hector.

I smell pine. And then chlorine. Sort of like a janitor's closet. Which does not sound like something that should make a girl swoon, but I am doing exactly that.

"Do you want to—" Hector asks, but before he can finish his question, the dance music fades and the Torino's DJ announces that she's taking a thirty-minute break. We aren't to worry, she assures us, because while she is gone, we'll be entertained by two fabulous, uh, entertainments. We watch her search for the night's schedule and then read from it. "First up, all the way from Walpole, the Lloyd Dobler Octet!"

Lights blaze at the front of the room, illuminating a shallow stage and blinding a row of trench coat–wearing teens holding old-fashioned boom boxes over their heads. One of them—a girl, it looks like, though it is hard to tell in the bright stage light—sets down her boom box, grabs a microphone, and begins an impressive measure of beat-boxing. A second later, the others have microphones, too, and are a cappella-ing the hell out of a song I don't recognize.

"'In Your Eyes.' It's from *Say Anything*. Classic eighties teen romance flick," Ellie says with admiration.

There is much to admire. The Doblers sound great, and although a decent portion of the Torino's occupants are now busy with minefield-appropriate activities, the rest offer an enthusiastic response to the Doblers' performance.

"We are the Lloyd Dobler Octet," says one of the trench-coated. He wears glasses, the glare off which is as dazzling as Aunt Carole's disco wreath. "Sorry there are only seven of us tonight. James had a wrestling match in Warsaw."

Someone in the crowd yells, "Vikings rule!" which earns almost as much applause as the Doblers' first number. The beatbox girl takes this as a sign to start their next song, a classic Joan Jett tune that actually has a few people returning to the dance floor.

Ellie snaps my suspenders. "I'm going to make sure the projector's ready," she says.

When Ellie leaves, Hector asks me if I'm nervous. The Doblers are really jamming now, and in order to be heard Hector has to lean close. *In a world where a kindhearted boy and a girl in a Santa hat* . . . do what, I wonder?

I turn my head to reply. Hector's lips are inches from

mine. They are very nice lips. And they are getting—are they getting?—I think they are getting closer to mine.

Stomach flips, knees wobble, chlorine overtakes the pine. Do what? Faint, maybe.

Hector catches me by the elbow. "Are you okay?" he asks. "Francie? Are you okay?"

Am I okay? I am not okay. Someone who was okay would have kissed Hector Ramirez on his very nice lips. I have not done that. I have, instead, stopped breathing. I make myself breathe. "I'm nervous," I say. "Just . . . nervous." I let him believe that my nerves are about the speech and not about the possibility that he was going to kiss me. A possibility, which, if it was once real, now seems to have vanished.

Hector is talking. I try to pay attention. "It's no different than in Ms. Colando's class," he is saying.

I make myself nod. Ms. Colando sometimes has us read our exploration pages aloud for everyone. In fact, tomorrow morning our group is scheduled to read in front of the rest of the class—not that I've had time to write a single exploratory word, but still, I know when it is due. "You're right. If I'm not nervous about tomorrow, I shouldn't be nervous tonight, right?" I pull myself together enough to meet Hector's eyes. He looks surprised. And maybe a little worried. About me, I think. This sweet boy is worried about me.

"We have to read our mythology responses in class *tomorrow*?" asks Hector.

Or maybe he is worried about his homework.

"What?" I ask. "Um . . . it's a B week. Yes."

"Not Tuesday?"

"Tomorrow. Friday," I confirm.

"Tomorrow," Hector says.

The shortest Dobler introduces another song, which she says will be the last of their set. Even a cappella, I recognize the first seven notes. The Clash. "Should I Stay or Should I Go."

Hector says what I am thinking: "Good question."

When the Doblers finish their song, their answer to its question is clear and they vacate the stage. Instantly, the room goes dark and a chorus of whistles and *whoo-ooo*s begin. Instrumental Christmas music fills the room. "Up on the Housetop." On a screen that had been the backdrop for the Lloyd Dobler Octet is a close-up of a pile of letters addressed in kid scrawl. A second later, the perfect voice-over voice of Hector Ramirez rumbles through the room.

You know Dasher and Dancer and Prancer and Vixen, he says. *You know about Hermie and Frosty and the gang of elves who make toys. You might think you know the whole story. But what you don't know is the carefully hidden truth about the real workers of the Christmas trade. The unseen, unsung heroes. Tonight, we introduce you to one of them. For security reasons, we will not use her name. We will call her only . . . Santa's Intern.*

The film runs. It is sweet and funny and the people

who are actually watching laugh. Of course a lot of people aren't actually watching. A lot of people are ordering food or making out in the minefield or getting some fresh air in the parking lot outside. But the people who do stay and watch laugh. And cheer. And they seem to be moved, at least a little bit, when they hear me talk about Olivia. Ellie runs that part—the Olivia story—over the footage she took of me outside the Tree Shed looking cold and small and lonely. Thankfully the film cuts then to some ridiculous clips of me struggling into my suspenders while Hector's voice sums up the various indignities of the Intern job. *It is worth it,* he tells the audience at the end of the film, *for the joy of giving. For the children. For Santa.* The audience applauds during the credits. They applaud even louder when the stage lights go on and I pick up a mic. There is even a little hooting, though I am not entirely sure it is supportive.

I thank Ellie for the film, thank people for coming. I remind them about Olivia and what we're here to raise money for. The lights are not only blinding, they are egg-fryingly hot and I can feel myself sweating under my Santa hat. "If you've got a little extra change at the end of the night," I say, wrapping it up as quickly as I can, "consider dropping it in the donation box by the door. It won't cost you much, and it could make a big difference to a kid like Olivia and a family in need."

There is applause, even from the minefield—though probably because they have sensed that this is the end of my speech and their work can now continue without distraction.

I step offstage, pull off my Santa hat, and loosen my tie. DeKieser stops me. "You have to, like, stay in character and everything if we're going to raise whatever money and stuff."

I put the hat back on. "I'm hot," I tell her.

"Now that she's a celebrity, she's all full of herself." I feel a hand on my back, then a finger tracing my suspenders. "Not that I disagree." A dimpled boy steps around to my side. Sam Spinek. "You do look pretty hot in those shorts." I shrug his hand off me, just as Hector arrives with Alice. He looks at the spot where Sam's hand was and I can't help wondering if he thinks I wanted it there. *I didn't,* I want to tell him. *I don't.* But what if he wasn't wondering? Or what if he was relieved to see it? What if he thinks that I didn't kiss him because I wanted to kiss Sam? Or, even more likely, what if he doesn't care?

"You did great." Alice hugs me. DeKieser does too. Sam looks like he's going to hug me, but then DeKieser grabs Kelsey's hand and says, "We should all, like, dance."

Sam nods. Hector doesn't. Instead he holds up his phone. "My brother's in the parking lot," he says to DeKieser. "I have to go."

He has to go? But wasn't the plan that his brother was going to pick him up at eleven o'clock? Wasn't he going to leave at closing like the rest of us?

"Homework," he says.

"Oh," I say. "Yeah. Of course."

I watch him go. So does Alice. "Weird," she says.

It's not weird. I'm weird. I thought he was trying to kiss me and I got weird and The Clash gave him a choice and he chose go.

"Were we going to dance?" asks Sam.

Alice nods. She doesn't know who this dimpled boy is yet. I should tell her, but I can't. I'm hot and I'm sweating and sick to my stomach and I have to get out of here.

"I need fresh air," I tell her. "I'll join you in a minute."

Before anyone can follow me, I'm in the Torino parking lot—just in time to see the taillights of Hector's brother's car pulling out onto the street.

32

"Hey," shouts somebody in the lot. "It's that elf girl."

I whip around, but before I can shout my correction, it is taken care of. "She's an intern, idiot." Gunther Hobbes, standing with a small group of puckheads in front of the yellow light of the Torino sign. He sticks out his tongue in greeting.

"The elf girl is the tongue girl?" asks the shouter.

Gunther nods, then waves me over. "That was a funny movie," he says. He holds out a beer. *BEER,* it says on the side.

"Isn't it alcohol-free teen night?" That's what's printed on the sign they are standing in front of: ALCOHOL-FREE TEEN NIGHT AT THE TORINO.

"It's Teen Night at the Torino," says Gunther. "In the parking lot, it's just regular old night."

He pops the cap. Hands the *BEER* to me.

"I'm on duty," I say, but I'm hot and sweaty and Hector Ramirez—who may or may not have been about to kiss me just twenty minutes ago—has decided it would be more fun to go home and do homework than be around me for one second longer. I take a deep swig.

Oh, holy night.

This is not my first drink or anything. I've tasted beer before. I've had wine at Thanksgivings and some champagne at Alice's aunt's baby shower. But this? This is foul. Disgusting. Unswallowable. I hold it in my mouth, thrust the bottle back at Gunther, and make like I've got urgent intern business inside. Once there, I have to dart through the dancers and dodge two minefield grinners before I reach the Torino restroom, the door to which is, of course, locked. Awful, funky, fetid swill! If I swallow it, I'll hurl, of this I am certain. I spy an exit door at the back of the hallway, push through it, and find myself in a small side parking lot where I can finally spew the nasty stuff onto an undeserving hedge. "Sorry," I tell the bush.

"You okay?" asks a voice. A boy's voice. I turn around.

It's a Dobler. The one with the glasses.

I wipe my mouth with my hand and nod. My mouth hasn't recovered enough to speak.

"You need anything?" he asks.

I need many things. A life. A spine. Four thousand dollars, a tank of gas, and a map to Arizona. "A toothbrush and a family-size tube of Crest," I say.

The Dobler pulls a pack of gum from his trench coat pocket and hands it to me.

"Thanks," I say. "I owe you."

"Really?" He studies my outfit. "Can I ask you a question? No offense or anything," he says. "But are you drunk?"

I shake my head.

"Not even a little?"

"I had a sip of *BEER* beer."

The Dobler wrinkles his nose. "How did that go?"

I wave a hand toward the bush. "Tastes like reindeer piss smells."

This makes the Dobler laugh. Me too, a little. "So, what are you?" he asks. "One of Santa's elves?"

"Intern!" How can this still be unclear to people? "I am Santa's freaking Intern," I tell him. "Did you not see the film?"

"Sorry. I must have been out here at the time. Sometimes I get nervous after a gig."

This surprises me. "After?" I ask.

"After. Before. During."

I shove the gum wrapper in my pocket and hand him back the pack. Cinnamon. The gum is cinnamon. "Thanks," I say again.

"You're welcome." The Dobler adjusts his glasses. He looks at my outfit again and he must decide it's okay. "You, uh, wouldn't want to see our tour bus, would you?"

"The Lloyd Dobler Octet has a tour bus?"

"It's really more of a van. Actually, it's Donnie's dad's Subaru, but I don't have much success asking girls if they want to see my friend's dad's Subaru."

"Do you have much success with the tour bus offer?" I ask.

"Not really," says the Dobler. "But it's a less humiliating request."

I nod. "I get that."

The Dobler nods too, and we chew our cinnamon gum together for a few minutes. "So," he says finally. "I'm guessing no to the Subaru, then?"

"No. Thank you. But don't feel bad. You're not missing out on much," I tell him.

"Now, I doubt that."

"No, really," I say, leaning resignedly against the Torino wall. "I'm a novice. I've never kissed anyone. Not really. I mean, I've kissed one person."

"Yeah?" he says.

"It didn't go well." I can't believe I'm telling him this. I didn't even swallow any of that *BEER* beer. It's just, it's kind of dark out here and this boy is a semianonymous Dobler and, I don't know. It feels private. Like a confessional.

"Was the guy—should I assume it was a guy?"

"A guy. A boy. He's inside there," I say, thumping the wall of the Torino.

"Was he a good guy? Someone you really liked?"

I look out into the dark of the parking lot, avoiding this kind Dobler's face and preserving the confessional feel. "He wasn't," I say. "He isn't. I didn't—not really—and I don't."

"Then it doesn't count."

I look at the boy's face again, wanting to be sure he's not joking. "It doesn't?"

"It only counts when you say it counts."

"So if I kissed you right now it wouldn't count."

"That'd be for you to decide," he says.

At first, I laugh. He's kind of charming, this Dobler boy. I bet he gets more Subaru visitors than he's letting on. In fact, I bet he's quite an experienced kisser. In fact . . . an impulsive idea springs to mind—but I fight the impulse long enough to consider things carefully.

"Dobler," I say. "May I call you Dobler?"

"It's Anthony, but I'm flexible."

"What I want, Dobler, is a kiss. One decent kiss. And then an evaluation."

"An evaluation?"

"One to ten rating. Maybe a few constructive comments."

"On your kissing?"

"On my kissing."

He considers the offer. "I could do that," he says. "Sure. Anything to help." The Dobler steps toward me.

"Uh, actually, wait," I say, suddenly nervous. *Think this through, Francie.* "I . . . I have a few more questions."

"Sure," he says. "Of course. Questions."

I think of all the things they warned us about in ninth-grade Health class. "Do you have herpes?" I ask.

"No."

"Cold sores of any kind?"

"No."

"Any history of sexually transmitted diseases?"

"None. I'm fully vaccinated, too, if you're interested."

"Good to know," I say. "Also, you understand what I'm after here? One kiss. This is not a flirtation. I'm not leading you on. I don't want to make out or date or marry you or anything in between."

"Completely understood."

"I'm not committing to or promising anything beyond this one kiss—that has to be perfectly clear."

"I have some of the band's performance contracts in the Subaru. I could make a few adjustments. Sign something if you—"

"Not necessary. I don't need a contract. I just need . . . I just need you to understand what I'm after. And I want to be fair to you. I want you to know—"

"Your terms are accepted. Shall we proceed?"

I nod and take out my gum. The Dobler does the same.

He moves closer. His eyes are green behind his glasses. He lifts his hand. "Can I . . . is it okay if I touch your cheek?"

"Is that standard?" I ask. I've seen a lot of kisses in movies and it does seem to happen often.

"No extra charge. And it helps with the aim."

I nod. "Okay," I say. "Okay. Should I put my hand on your face too?"

"You can, but things get a little boxed in that way," he says.

"Then you do it and I'll just . . ." What will I do? Where do my hands go? I put them in my Corporate Christmas shorts pockets.

The Dobler puts a hand on my cheek. It is warm. The night, I realize, is cool. Cold, even.

"Good?" he asks.

"Good," I say.

His face draws closer to mine. His head tilts just a little to the right and I tilt mine a little too.

And then his lips are on mine and they are warm and cinnamony. Soft. No tongue. Nice. And warm and soft and good and something I could keep doing for a while.

So we do that for a while. And I realize that I'm not really sure what constitutes a single kiss because what we do feels sort of like it could be a series of kisses or one long kiss or some combination of that. But why quibble? It is nice. Eventually he takes his lips from mine and looks me in the eye.

"One to ten?" he asks.

I'm almost afraid to speak. "One to ten," I confirm.

"Well," he says, "it started as a five."

"A five," I say. A five? I *am* bad at this. I am *terrible* at this. A five?

"You were a little stiff. A little . . . not-quite-in-the-room. But by the end, I'd say a solid eight."

An eight sounds better. Possibly even good. I check.

"An eight is good, right?" His hand is not on my face anymore.

"An eight is good. Very good. Especially considering the mitigating factors."

Mitigating factors? He's grading on a curve! There *is* something wrong with me. My lips are weird or I breathe funny or—

"Kissing is always better when there's a little bit of hope in the air. When the kiss matters to both parties," he says.

"When they like each other," I say.

"Or they think they might, when there's potential. Faith in a possible future. Then . . . ," he says. "Then you've got a kiss of consequence."

A kiss of consequence. I get that. I think.

"Under proper conditions, you'd get a ten for sure."

"Really?"

He nods. "You know, if you decided to go out with me, like on a real date, I think we might be able to create those conditions."

This bespectacled Dobler is cute. And kind. And funny. And he's here. He's not at home pretending to have suddenly remembered a homework assignment because some idiot girl freaked out instead of kissing him back. But . . .

"There's someone else in your sights," he says. "Ah, well. 'Here's looking at you, kid.'" He raises an imaginary drink in my direction.

"That's from a movie, isn't it?"

"*Casablanca,*" he says. "Bogart. 1942. Bogart says it to Bergman as he sends her away to be with—"

I cut him off. "You're the one who thought up the name of your band, aren't you?"

"The Lloyd Dobler Octet? It's a reference to *Say Anything.* Classic eighties teen—"

"Uh-huh," I say. I grab his hand. "Come with me."

"Yeah?" he asks. "You change your mind?"

"I want you to meet someone. Someone who just might be interested in the proper conditions of which you speak."

"Really?" he says.

"Just don't ask her about the Subaru, okay?"

Ellie and the Dobler—Anthony—hit it off instantly.

When the lights go up at eleven, I catch sight of them near the mistletoe minefield. The kiss I witness is short, not more than a peck, and yet I intuit a kiss of consequence. My suspicions are confirmed when Anthony turns to leave. He sees me watching, mouths a *thank-you,* and holds up both hands. A ten. The look on Ellie's face suggests she concurs.

"You're just making everybody's Christmas dreams come true, aren't you?" says Alice.

"Not everybody's." I still am not sure whether Hector wanted to kiss me in the first place, but if he did, if he tries again, I'll be ready. "But I'm working on it," I tell her.

33

DECEMBER 16

After school the next day, I go home to change into my Intern uniform (which Gram has washed for me during the day), grab a brownie off the kitchen counter, and head over to the shop. The flow of letters seems to be slowing. On Tuesday, Bryan had only half a box for me to do, and after Ellie and Hector were done filming the Tree Shed and went home, I got to spend most of my shift in the aisles, straightening displays and sorting ornaments and helping customers. I expect today will be much the same, but when I get to my Intern desk, Bryan is waiting for me. In her hand is one of DeKieser's Torino flyers. "Carole would like to see you in her office." She turns on a robotic heel. "Follow me."

"I know where Carole's office is," I tell her, but it

doesn't change anything. I guess once your programming is engaged, there's no altering your path—a thought I find personally disconcerting as well, for some reason.

It feels to me like the Miata is the answer. Sunshine-yellow autonomy. The world will open up to me. I'll have choices. I'll get to hang out with Alice when I want to. Maybe even with Hector. If *he* wants to.

I'm not sure that he does want to, though. This morning in Mythology Today he hardly said hello. He kept his eyes on his paper, silently reading—or pretending to read?—his essay. I tried to catch his eye, but then Ms. Colando called me to the front of the room to read mine, "Nobody Expects Coal." I had to get up early this morning to write it and I have to admit, it wasn't my best. Who is at their best at five a.m.? After a night of alcohol-free teen fun? After a night of losing more than four hundred fifty dollars from their Miata fund? After Dobler kissing? After being too afraid to kiss a fine-shouldered boy who may or may not have wanted to kiss me? It was hard to keep my eyes open as I wrote it. It was hard to keep them open as I read it aloud in Mythology Today. And a minute or so into the next reader—DeKieser on why college brochures never have pictures with snow in them—I stopped even trying and fell asleep at my desk for the rest of the period.

"Here she is," says Bryan. She holds Carole's office door open for me.

"Frankincense," says Aunt Carole. "Have a seat."

I follow directions.

"Can you explain this?" She gestures toward Bryan.

"Cyborg?" I say. "Bionics? Secret government plot to infiltrate the high-stakes world of the tinsel trade?"

Aunt Carole is not amused. "The flyer."

"It was a fundraiser. For a food pantry."

She picks a slip of paper off her desk. "Your schedule request indicates you wanted last night off for a school-related project. So you lied?"

"It *was* a school-related project. The film—it was a project by my friend Ellie. And I was in it."

"While you were in your uniform," says Carole. "While you were representing this business. Without permission or prior approval."

How does she know all this? "It was for charity," I say.

"I am the head of Marketing," says Carole. "I make the charity decisions. We are already busy with a number of charities. The Hollydale Public Library. Toys for Tots. The children's party at the hospital."

"I thought we weren't doing that this year," I say. Every year since I can remember, Grampa Chris or later, Dad, has played Santa at the holiday party in the children's wing of Grace Memorial Hospital. But also every year since I can remember, Mom and Dad go on an overnight trip to Chicago for their wedding anniversary. It's the one concession Christmas has to make to their non-Christmas lives. They've never missed it. And since this is their twentieth anniversary, they are not about to change that, even if it does mean letting some other Santa have the hospital gig. In fact, given how hard they've both been working, they seem doubly eager to go. I almost tripped over their suitcase in the hall this morning. I really do need to learn to turn on more lights.

"I didn't mean us, of course," says Aunt Carole. "I helped the hospital make other arrangements. That itself was a charitable act. Also, none of your business." She seems even more short-tempered than usual. I notice a copy of the *Hollydale Daily* open on her desk. There has been another letter to the editor, this one in support of the wreath. It is signed "Lover of all that is Holly and Jolly," but the text of the letter is full of spite and disdain, and though the writer swears that just looking at the wreath as she drives by puts jingle bells in her heart, I am pretty certain that the actual sound is closer to the rattle of bracelets.

"And I see here that you have asked for more time off tomorrow?" She waves another schedule request.

"We're delivering the food and the books to the Elf Shelf," I tell her. "Alice is doing a story about it and she wants me there for photos. It could be good publicity. Great publicity. I mean, a story in the *Daily* and all those happy people and"—I'm babbling now. It's just that I promised Alice I'd be there and Hector got his brother to drive and—"people are hungry and—"

"What time?" Carole interrupts.

"For dropping off the food? Hector's brother is picking

us up at noon to get the food from the Torino and then we'll all drive to the Elf Shelfs and take some pictures and—"

"So you'll be occupied in the afternoon?" says Carole. I see her make eye contact with Bryan, who writes something in her notebook. She's docking me Pillar Points, I can tell. I wish I knew how many I had, whether it was even worth working the way I have been. I would so love to get a glimpse of that notebook. But since I can't, groveling seems best. "I can work the salesfloor in the morning," I say. "I can come in at seven thirty and help Dottie before the store opens if you—"

Rattling bracelets. "Fine," says Carole. She looks at Bryan again, then back at me. "But as long as you are going to be out in the world representing the shop, you might as well take the entire afternoon. Be visible. Volunteer. Pose for pictures. Lots of pictures. Don't rush back."

Bryan nods.

"Are you sure? I mean, Mom and Dad won't be back from Chicago until late tomorrow night. Uncle Jack has plans. Dottie might need—"

"You are not indispensable, Frances," says Carole. "We have many employees—permanent, non-probationary employees—who can run this store just fine for a day." She glances at Bryan, who has her pen poised above her notebook, waiting, I assume, for the go-ahead to dock another point.

"Okay," I say. "Good, I mean."

"Is that all?" asks Carole. She looks as if that is not all. As if that should not be all.

"Thank you?" I say.

A small smile lifts the corner of Carole's face. It looks uncomfortable there, as if her mouth is out of practice.

"All afternoon. And don't hurry back. Go play with your friends afterward," she says. I study her face. I think she actually means it. Holy moly, a Christmas miracle! "Go to a movie. Go ice-skating. I hear the rink is open tomorrow for free skate. I used to love that when I was your age."

When she was my age. Sometimes I forget that Carole was ever my age. That she grew up in the very house in which we're now sitting. That she worked in the Holiday Shop just like I did. That Grampa Chris was her dad and her boss and that maybe she was saving up for something she really wanted. That maybe, once, she was a little bit like me.

Nah.

Back at my Intern desk I find only a shoebox full of letters, most of them the kind I could reply to in my sleep. In fact, I nod off a couple of times while writing.

Dear Deedee:

Thanks for your letter.

Dear Kiddo:

I've let Santa know about the baseball mitt.

Dear Dewayne:

I'm glad you've been good this week.

Dear Rain:

Karate class sounds like a kick.

A harried-looking woman with three kids parks them in front of me before heading off to Gift Wrap. "Stay with the elf," she tells them, despite my prominently displayed *Santa's Intern* mailbox. "Ask her some questions."

Their questions are ones I've encountered in the letters too. How did you get your job? Do you get paid? Is it fun?

Rigorous application and interview process.

I get paid in the smiles of children.

Look at all these letters! Doesn't this look like fun?

"Where'd you get those cool shorts?" I look up from my letter writing. Standing behind a pair of my smaller inquisitors is a stocky blond guy in a Hollydale Vikings hockey jersey.

"Gunther Hobbes. Star forward. Fashion critic," I say. His forehead wrinkles. He has forgotten that he was also the one to notice my candy-cane skirt. I, of course, have not forgotten. "The shorts are standard-issue intern wear.

We all received them after orientation. The tie, however, is my own choice."

"It's pretty," says one of the children.

"Thank you." I ask the kid her name and she tells me it is Stella. "I'll make sure Santa hears about your superior manners, Stella."

"You should tell him that guy was rude too." Stella scowls at Gunther.

"Good idea," I say. I take up a scrap piece of paper. *Stella has good manners,* I write. *Gunther Hobbes is rude.*

Stella's mom shows up then and herds her children toward the cashier. "Wave goodbye to the elf," she tells them. I bang my intern mailbox at her, but she doesn't notice.

"Coach said I could find some ornaments with hockey stuff on them here," says Gunther. "Do you know where those are?"

I could tell him, but he'd never find them—and not just because he has the intellectual capability of a cereal box. The Hollydale Holiday Shop has thousands of ornaments, arranged by theme and interest. There are more than one hundred dog-breed ornaments alone. The sports-themed decorations are toward the back, wedged between College and Popular Culture. Hockey, while big at Hollydale High School, is not nearly as popular in Indiana as basketball or even football. The glass pucks and tiny goalie masks (cross merchandised in the Creepy Christmas aisle) can be tough to spot. I lead Gunther there, then return to my desk. Somehow, in the less than three minutes it took to get Gunther to Sports, Bryan has whisked away all of my finished letters and refilled the shoebox. Sisyphus was a wuss.

> *Dear Chanel:*
> *Santa will be glad to hear you did so well*
> *on your spelling test.*

> *Dear Crosse:*
> *Santa will be glad to hear you're doing*
> *better in school.*

> *Dear Dayo:*
> *Snowmen are nice. They can be a little*
> *frosty until you get to know them, but then*
> *they warm up.*

"Do that one next." Gunther is back. He's got a basket with three Ho Ho Hockey bulbs and a couple of glass pucks in it. "The one in the orange envelope."

There is a tall orange envelope among the remaining letters. The return address says "Hobbes Heating and Cooling."

"Did you write Santa a letter, little boy?"

"I didn't write it, my sister did," says Gunther. "I want to see what she wrote."

"I'm afraid Santa's Intern has signed a strict confidentiality agreement. If I showed you, one of the North Pole's elite team of elf assassins would take me out and—" I draw my finger across my neck ominously.

"I need to see it, okay?" There's something almost human in the way he says it. "Christmas was my mom's thing. My dad, he pays for everything, but if there's going to be Christmas at my house now, I have to do it." He lifts the shopping basket of puck ornaments. "Gordie wouldn't let me see her list when she was writing it. She's a good kid. She deserves a good Christmas, okay?"

He says this like I'd know what happened to his mom, why his dad is now responsible for Christmas, but I don't. I'm not going to ask him either. But I take the orange envelope from my stack and open it. I don't hand the letter to him, but I flatten it out so he can read over my shoulder. If, you know, he can read. "Don't let the elf assassins catch you looking," I tell him. I take Aunt Carole's sunglasses out of my pocket and put them on, like this somehow means I'm doing something sneaky. But really, it feels like maybe Gunther is the one who needs privacy and this is the only way I can give it to him.

"Oh no!" says Gunther. "She wants the purple Fairy Ninja Twin! I got her the pink one. The lady at the store said all the girls Gordie's age want the pink one. I should have known. She's just not a pink kind of kid." There is a real tenderness in his voice. He loves his sister. Gunther Hobbes loves someone.

"Thanks, Francie," he says. I didn't even know that he knew my name.

I shrug an "it's nothing" shrug and adjust my suspenders.

"No, really. Thanks," he says. "If those elf assassins come after you, let me know."

"How about you just stop harassing me at school, huh?"

It takes a minute for him to figure out what I'm talking about. "You mean . . ." He sticks his tongue out. "Ramirez told us he didn't want to see us do it again."

"He did?"

"Yeah. So we stopped doing it in class, but then Spinek said you liked it. That you like the attention." Gunther looks puzzled. "It really bugs you?"

"What do you think?" I don't want to talk about this anymore. I pick up my pen and some intern stationery.

Dear Gordie, I write.

"Tell her she'll get the purple Fairy Ninja Twin. No, wait. Tell her she'll get both of the Fairy Ninja Twins."

"Santa doesn't make promises," I tell Gunther.

"He doesn't?"

"You never know what's going on in a kid's life. You don't know if they've got a parent who is anti–video game or who doesn't have the cash for what they want or—"

"Who's going to get the pink Fairy Ninja Twin instead. I get it. But she's getting them both. I can promise you that."

If this wasn't Gunther Hobbes, I'd be tempted to pat his arm and tell him I believe him. Okay, it is Gunther Hobbes and I do that anyway.

He stands behind me as I write another line.

"And tell her to stop snooping in my room, would you? I've got all her presents in my extra hockey bag and I'm afraid she'll find them."

I tell Gordie that Santa sees her when she's sneaking.

"Thanks," says Gunther. "Hey, I'm sorry about the—" He looks like he's going to stick out his tongue again, but I stop him.

"Gunther, I'd really like never to see that again."

Gunther nods. "Okay," he says. "Okay." He turns to leave, then stops. "Hey, Francie? Just cuz I've been a jerk, doesn't mean Gordie. . . . Could you just . . . could you make her letter a good one?"

He leaves then. I write the letter. It isn't bad.

34

DECEMBER 17

Alice and I are standing in the parking lot behind the North Pole waiting for Hector and Luis to pick us up and take us to the Torino, where DeKieser has been boxing up the food donations. It is cold and windy and for the first time since becoming Santa's Intern I am grateful for my Santa hat. I am also grateful for the big puffy coat I am wearing. It is the kind that looks like a sleeping bag with arms, and while I would never wear it to school, it is the perfect thing for keeping warm when you are sporting Corporate Christmas shorts.

The weather forecast is for snow this evening, but I'll believe it when I see it, as the radio weather guy has forecasted snow twice earlier this season and we haven't seen a flake. Besides the weather guy, that is.

Alice is typing away on her phone, using it to start a draft of her story for the *Hollydale Daily*. She has to turn it in this evening and, if everything goes right, it will run in the Tuesday edition. "Do you remember how much all those copies of *Charlotte's Web* cost?" she asks me.

How could I forget? "Eight hundred and seventy-four dollars," I say.

She warms her thumbs with her breath. Types *Teens from local high schools raised $874.*

Most of which came from one teen in particular, I would text if I could. A teen who is not as far along in her quest for sunshine-yellow autonomy as she had hoped to be by this time.

A gust of wind threatens to take my Santa hat and I try to imagine the warmer summer breezes that will accompany my top-down convertible drives once the Miata is mine. And I learn to drive.

Hector's brother's hatchback pulls up, but it is not Luis who is driving. Hector is.

"You have your license?" Alice asks as we pile into the back seat.

"I have a permit," says Hector. "My birthday's in January."

"This boy needs a lot of practice," says Luis.

Luis is not kidding. Hector's hands are firm at nine and three on the steering wheel, but his speed is erratic and at every red light or stop sign he halts the car a good ten feet before he is supposed to, creeps slowly up to the real stop line, and halts the car again. Each time he looks to his brother for approval, receives a nod, then takes off again a little too fast—a speed he will overcorrect for moments later. As a result, the drive that should take us fifteen minutes takes almost twice that, but nobody says anything. After all, none of us even has a permit.

When we finally reach the Torino we discover that the staff and clientele have been adding to the food donations we collected on Thursday and there are now more boxes of books and nonperishables than will fit in the hatchback, so we have to shove some of the boxes on the floor of the car too. As a result, DeKieser and Alice and I squish together crisscross applesauce, our legroom taken up by canned goods and stories of terrific pigs.

After a long wait for Hector to find the appropriate space between oncoming cars, we pull out into traffic and head for the first of the two Elf Shelfs. When we arrive, Alice and I go inside to meet with a man that Alice's notes say is Charlie. Our meeting is short. Charlie is busy. The entire food pantry is busy. I spy a couple of girls in the nine-to-twelve-year-old range. Might one of them be Olivia?

"Has either of you read *Charlotte's Web*?" I ask.

The younger one admits to having seen the movie. The other one is scared of pigs. Neither is named Olivia. Alice tells them to stay put and we'll give them a free copy of the book for their very own.

Their mother looks wary. "You aren't from some cult

or something, are you? You haven't rewritten the story and filled it with references to your own personal prophet?"

"It's just the regular *Charlotte's Web*," I promise, and then leave to tell Hector to drive around the back of the pantry to drop off the food and most of the books. Charlie wants me to bring one of the book boxes in now and set it at the register where his volunteers will be able to hand one out to every family that comes through.

Alice stays inside, hoping to ask the mom a few more questions for her story.

When I come back in, I give a copy of *Charlotte's Web* to the girls and hand the rest to Charlie. Soon I'm joined by Hector, DeKieser, and Luis.

"Excuse me." A volunteer pushes past us with a crate full of milk cartons. Several people take cartons from her before she even arrives at the refrigerator.

"Are there always this many people here?" Luis asks Charlie, who shakes his head.

"We serve a lot of families, but what you're seeing here is the combination of Christmas and an impending snowstorm."

"Can you, like, use any help or whatever?"

"I've got plenty of volunteers now," says Charlie. "Christmas brings out the best in people. When I need help is in February, when the Christmas spirit is gone and the New Year's resolutions have faded. Then I need volunteers—dependable ones who actually commit to a schedule."

DeKieser doesn't look at him. Alice and Hector and I don't either. We are teenagers without cars. We can't commit to anything that requires transportation without talking to our parents. Silently I vow that when I get the Miata I will volunteer at the Elf Shelf once a week. Luis, though, takes a brochure off the counter and tells Charlie he'll call him in late January, once he's sure of next semester's schedule.

Charlie shakes Luis's hand as a family steps up to the counter. Another girl of Olivia's age stands behind her parents. Hector hands her a book. "For you," he says. "Compliments of Santa's Intern."

"Say thank you, Quinn," says the mom.

This girl is not Olivia either.

"We're in the way here," says Luis. "Vamos."

The second Elf Shelf is much like the first. We drop off books and food. Alice remembers that she needs a picture of me so I hand my sleeping bag coat to DeKieser, hold up a book and a can of soup, and pose with the second Elf Shelf's version of Charlie. It is all over in ten minutes.

"It was, like, a good thing we did," says DeKieser as Hector crawls the hatchback out of the lot. "People needed that food and stuff. And the kids were glad to get, like, their own books."

Fully stopped, Hector replies, "I just wish we could be sure that Olivia will get one."

DeKieser doesn't say anything to that, but I can tell she wishes so too. Alice might feel that way, but she's not listening to us. She is using her phone to type up her *Hollydale Daily* story.

"You do what you can do," says Luis, reminding me of my Grampa Chris.

There's only so much you can do, he'd tell his students. *All you have is a few minutes. You can't hand each kid a new bike or cure their cold or fix any of the other things that might be going on in their life. But for a few precious minutes, you can give that child your full attention. You can let them know they are worthy of that time, worthy of love.* And then, quietly, so his students would have to lean in to hear, he'd say, *Children don't believe in Santa because of the boots or the hat or the belly or the beard. Children believe in Santa because they know Santa believes in them.*

35

After a half hour of Hector driving, the car pauses, crawls forward a few feet, then stops for real at the back door of the North Pole. Despite Hector's speed—or lack thereof—our deliveries have taken a lot less time than we anticipated.

Hector doesn't need to be at the Library Fundraising Christmas Tree Lot for a couple of hours. DeKieser's mom is still doing her Christmas shopping. "You guys want to come in for cookies?" I ask.

Hector and Luis confer in Spanish. Luis does a lot of looking at me and giving Hector kid-brother nudges. Hector gets out of the car and says something else in Spanish to his brother, who has moved into the driver's seat. "Have faith," Luis says back.

"Cookies," says Alice. "And then you all have to shut up so I can write."

The breakroom is full of seasonal employees recovering from their time on the salesfloor. Gram has taken good care of them, though. In addition to whatever cookies are in the snowman, there are platters of brownies and bowls of fruit on the counter. We load up a plate with treats and I lead us to Snowflake, which should be empty and quiet enough for Alice to work in.

Snowflake is quiet. But it is not empty. Bryan is there, and so are three cardboard boxes. Big boxes. Big enough to hold a tree's worth of ornaments. Big enough to hold a disco door wreath, even.

"What's this?" I ask Bryan, but I don't really have to. I know. The boxes are full of letters. Letters to Santa's Intern. "Where did these come from?" I ask. "And don't say children."

"I was just leaving you a note." Bryan tears a page from her notebook and hands it to me. It is very thorough. It explains that there are a lot of letters and that Carole believes that the children who have written these letters deserve my reply before Christmas Eve.

I pull an envelope from the closest box. The postmark says December 7. "How long has this been here?" I ask. I pull another envelope from the box and another and another. December 10. December 12. "Why are they just sitting here? Why didn't you give these to me earlier?"

"Carole said not to overwhelm you," says Bryan. She

has noticed the edge in my voice. She sets down her notebook, I assume because her programming has warned her that I might attack and that she'll need her hands free for defense.

I fish out another letter. It is from a kid right here in Hollydale, postmarked December 8. *PLEASE WRITE BACK* is printed in desperate cherry crayon.

How many are there? Five hundred? A thousand? How many kids hoping to hear back from Santa's Intern? How many wanting to believe? How many now won't? Because there is no way I can answer all these letters in time. No way. Not even if Alice had time to help. Not even if Hector did. How could Aunt Carole ever expect me to finish all these boxes?

She can't. She doesn't. She expects me to fail. And for people to be mad. And for the Santa School to pay the price.

"Where is she?" I ask Bryan. Alice's eyebrows go into high alert—a warning not to do something wild and irreversible. I don't need a warning. It is my aunt who should be warned. "Where is Carole?"

"She's not here," says Bryan, inching toward the door. "She'll be back tonight. I think. Maybe." It is impressive how fast a robot can move when properly motivated. The door bangs shut behind her.

Nobody says anything. Alice, Hector, and DeKieser watch me warily. Finally, DeKieser breaks the silence. "That's, like, a lot of mail."

I circle the table. There are hundreds of letters. Impossible. Impossible. There is nothing I can do.

When I've almost completed the circuit, I see the notebook that Bryan has accidentally left behind. I wonder when Carole made her plan to ruin me? I bet it is in here—Bryan, I know, takes excellent notes. I grab the notebook to search for the proof, but stop on the open page. It is Bryan's daily to-do list. *Move letters to Snowflake,* it says, but this is not what has caught my eye. Up near the top of the page is another line with a box in front of it, neatly checked off. *Pick up Mr. McCaffery at airport.* McCaffery. I know that name. McCaffery . . . the name feels pink. Sticky, like marshmallow.

Brady McCaffery. Santa Slick.

"I have to go to the hospital," I say.

"What?" asks Alice.

Hector is instantly at my side. "Are you okay? Do you need to sit? Should we call an ambulance?"

In the moment that it took me to remember Santa Slick's real name is Brady McCaffery, Aunt Carole's evil plan has also become apparent. The Santa that she arranged to work the children's party at the hospital is Santa Slick. Bryan's to-do list confirms it. *Three p.m.,* it says, *Drop Mr. McCaffery at Grace.*

"Why is that so bad?" asks Hector when I explain. "The kids need a Santa, right?"

"It's not the kids she's thinking about." I tell him the holiday party at Grace Memorial is funded by a dozen of the county's largest and most important businesses—the Hollydale Mall, the Chrysler dealership, the local bookstore, Target—all of which hire Santas for the holidays. All of which get their Santa recommendations from Dad. All of which endorse our school and encourage potential Santas to take our classes. And all of which send their managers or CEOs or marketing people to the Grace Memorial children's Christmas party to see what their donations have enabled.

Carole wants them to see Santa Slick in action. She wants them to tell Dad just how great he is. She wants them to know that when Santa Slick takes over the school, things will actually be better than they were before. She is there, making promises, telling lies.

I check the time. The party started fifteen minutes ago. I can't stop Santa Brady McCaffery from slicking up Christmas, but I might be able to stop Aunt Carole from making her sales pitch and doing damage to Grampa Chris's school.

"I have to go to the hospital," I say again.

"So, you *do* want us to call an ambulance." Alice's eyebrows are sending *duh* signs now. "Francie, none of us can drive."

DeKieser tilts her head toward Hector. "He, like, can."

"*Like* is the operative word," says Alice. I know she's being snarky about Hector's driving skills, but she pretends she's not. "He only has a permit."

"I'd drive you anyway," he says. "But Luis wouldn't

let me drive without him and he's working the lot. I don't have access to a car."

Sweet golden autonomy. The Miata. "I do," I say.

Snowflake has a spare set of keys for each of the Christmas Shop buildings and it only takes a second to lift the garage key off its peg. Uncle Jack is ice-skating with a widow, I tell Hector. After that, he'll take her to dinner. Even if she's an early bird–special widow, there's no way Uncle Jack will be back before six. I grab Bryan's notebook in case there is any other information that can help me foil Aunt Carole, and from a cupboard I snatch an enormous, plush velvet bag ($27.95). "If anyone tries to stop us, we'll say Santa left this behind and we've got to bring it to him," I say.

"You think that will, like, work?" asks DeKieser.

"Trust me," I tell her. "I'm Santa's Intern."

36

The garage is dark. I flip on the lights and am halfway to Uncle Jack's tarp-covered Miata when I notice that the Miata is not there and the tarp is now tied over the bed of his pickup truck. The Miata, I understand, is on his widow date.

"You can drive a truck, right?"

Hector's face says he isn't sure, but when I take the keys from their wall peg, he opens his hand for them.

It turns out that Hector drives a truck about as well as he drives his brother's car, so it takes us three times as long to get to Grace Memorial as it should. Alice spends the time typing her *Daily* story on her phone and I flip through Bryan's notebook. Most of it is to-do lists and notes for letters to the editor that Carole is thinking about writing. There's also a section in it filled with interview questions and answers. It seems Bryan had to write a business biography of her mentor. I flip through the interview, too, most of which is pretty dull. Aunt Carole was born in Hollydale. She was a good student. She worked part-time at the shop all through high school.

Then, it looks like, Bryan must have asked her about why she moved to California. *By the time I was in high school, it was pretty clear Nicky was going to inherit the business. My father wasn't going to waste his time training a girl who could never be Santa Claus.* There's a note saying that Bryan asked her if she wanted to be Santa, but it looks like Aunt Carole didn't answer. Instead she started talking about marketing and margins and all the things she learned in business school and how somebody had to shake things up at the Holiday Shop or it would never grow in the way it should. Of course.

When Hector finally parks Uncle Jack's truck (at the back of the hospital lot, far away from the other cars) we pull our coats tight around us and dash inside.

I've been to this Christmas party before. It is on the third floor. There's a playroom just down the hall from the elevator and all the kids who are well enough to go to the party will meet Santa there. Kids who aren't well enough stay in their rooms and wait for Santa to visit them personally. The party is big and noisy and fun. The visits, I suspect, are not—but I'm not 100% sure of that. Grampa

Chris always visited those children on his own.

Nobody stops us at the entrance or at the elevators, and when we get off on the third floor we're far enough away from the nurse's station that nobody really notices us either. We look like we're here to visit a family member. Or Alice and DeKieser and Hector do. I look like Mrs. Claus's publicist.

"What now?" asks Alice. She's getting into the adventure of this and there's a hint of Miss Fisher in her voice.

Good question. What I want to do is bust into that Christmas party and confront Aunt Carole about her back-stabbing trickery and tell her she won't get away with it and wait until my dad hears. But even as I think this, I know what will happen. I'll tell Dad about Aunt Carole and then she will tell him her version of things and also how immature and impulsive and untrustworthy I am and he won't want to choose which story to believe and nothing will change. And Aunt Carole will ruin everything Grampa Chris worked so hard for.

Down the hallway, a door opens and a tall, white-haired, wrist-bangled woman steps into the hall. *Aunt Carole!* I shove my friends into a conveniently placed closet and pull the door shut behind us. It's dark and we're a little squished.

Alice's accent disappears. "Hector, your elbow is in my cleavage."

"Sorry," he says. It's too dark to be sure, but I imagine he is blushing. "Better?"

"No."

"Oh, that's, like, me, I think."

One of us finds a light switch. It is a linen closet we're in. Bedsheets and towels and those tie-in-the-back gowns are stacked on shelves. The light makes this apparent. It also makes apparent that everyone is looking expectantly at me.

"I wish my dad was here," I tell Alice.

"He wouldn't fit," says Hector.

"Why are, like, *we* here?" asks DeKieser.

I explain what I've been thinking, including the part about where my dad might not really see things my way. How it is possible that I may have acted impulsively. How I might need a quiet moment squished in a closet with three other teenagers in order to figure this out.

"What you really need is evidence," says Alice, full Miss Fisher now. "You need to catch her on film."

"That would be ideal," I admit. "But if she knew I was recording her she'd lie or pretend nothing was going on."

Alice strokes her chin and Miss Fisher–thinks about this for a second, but it is DeKieser who comes up with the plan. "You know, like, what if . . . ," she says.

DeKieser's plan, in short, is this: Alice and I will remain in the closet. She and Hector will go to the playroom and pretend to take video of the party but really, they'll be getting as close to Aunt Carole as possible, recording every word she says to the Santa-hiring business leaders of Hollydale,

Indiana. Then, when DeKieser's got the goods, she'll call me and Alice and we'll rush out of the closet, burst into the playroom, and stop Aunt Carole from whatever other evil deeds she has planned. The, like, thing is, DeKieser explains, it might look kind of suspicious or whatever if she just barges into a sick children's party without seeming to know any of the sick children. The thing is, she says again, it would be better if she, like, had a sick child with her.

"No way," says Hector.

"This evil Carole person would recognize Alice and Francie," says DeKieser.

"No way," says Hector again.

DeKieser shrugs. "Whatever. Ruin Christmas."

The Hollydale Holiday Shop stocks more than forty thousand individual items in any single Christmas season. Nearly every one of them has a customer I understand. I understand the lure of fairy lights, the religious connection to the things in the Nativity Showroom, the pressed-plastic ornaments for baby births and favorite television shows and professional sports teams. But there are always a few head-scratchers. For example, the three packs of holiday boxer briefs. Who, I have always wondered, actually wears Frosty the Snowman knickers? The answer, it turns out, is Hector Ramirez.

"You can put your shirt and pants in here." Alice hands him the Santa bag I brought from Snowflake. "Fine," says Hector, "but I'm wearing my boots. And my jacket." He pulls his leather jacket on over the bunny-covered hospital gown we have boosted from the linen closet shelves.

"That's good," says Alice. "Keep your sleeves pulled down and the jacket will hide where your ID band should be."

"I hope that's not all it hides." Hector wraps the gown tighter around his backside, which I have to admit looks as appealing in Frosty wear as it did in his jeans on Torino alcohol-free teen night.

"The Intern will tell Santa of your heroism on his behalf," says Alice.

"Thank you," I tell Hector.

"Ten minutes," says Hector.

"Ten minutes."

DeKieser and Hector sneak out into the hallway and shut the door behind them. A second later, the door opens and DeKieser reaches in to switch off the light. "You can, like, see the light," she explains. She shuts the door again and Alice and I are in the dark. As much as I love Alice, I can't help wishing, just for a second, that she was the one walking down the hall with DeKieser and Hector was still in here—though what I would do if I were really stuck in a darkened closet for ten minutes with Hector Ramirez is almost too embarrassing to contemplate.

"This is exciting," whispers Alice.

"I can't see your eyebrows. Are you being sarcastic?"

"No, it's really fun! It reminds me of playing hide-and-seek when we were little."

It reminds me of that too. The dark. The heart-pounding threat that you'd be found. The thrill when you were. The seemingly life-depending run for home safe.

"I miss that," says Alice. "And I miss you."

"I miss you too," I say back.

"It doesn't have to be this way, you know," says Alice.

"It does. If we turn on the light, some dedicated energy conservationist might notice and—"

"That's not what I mean," says Alice.

I know that is not what she means. I know that what she means is that we don't have to be apart so much. That I don't have to go to Hollydale High School. That I could go to Regina, Queen of Heaven like she does, and we could have classes together and ride the interfaith party bus together and everything would be like it used to be.

"I know it's not about the uniforms. I mean, look at you."

Neither of us can actually look at me in this dark closet, but I know what she means. "It's not about the uniforms," I admit.

"Is it about being Catholic? You don't *have* to even be Catholic to go to Regina. A lot of girls go there just for the education. We've got at least two agnostics in our class, and Lakshmi and Serena are Hindu, and who knows how many of us are closet atheists."

It feels like there is a joke to be made about closets, but I can't locate it in the dark.

"You believe in God, right?"

"Yes," I tell her.

"And you go to Mass with your family on Sundays."

"Yes," I say.

"So what's the problem?"

There are footsteps outside the closet. A woman's voice tells someone about a girl in 312 who should be on the Personal Visit from Santa list. We wait in silence until we're sure they've passed.

What *is* the problem? "Everybody was so . . . certain," I tell her. "When Grampa Chris died, everyone at the funeral and the wake and at school that fall was so certain about where he was and that he was in a better place and what exactly God meant for him."

"And you weren't," Alice says. Not like a question.

"I needed to figure it out for myself. I needed—I *need*—the space to figure out what I believe."

"You know I don't believe everything, right? Like DeKieser. I know what the church says about gay people, but I don't believe any of that. And—by the way—neither do a couple of the nuns."

Alice has told me this before, and I've told her that I believe her. I tell her this again. I also tell her that while I admire her for finding the space within her school, I can't yet. "It would feel like a lie."

"What about Santa, then?" asks Alice.

"I'm sure he'll visit that girl. Even Santa Slick wouldn't ignore a sick child."

"Francie, cut it out. Stop pretending you don't know

what I mean when you do. What about *you* and Santa? You know there's no Santa. You know there's no dude in a red wool suit running a toy empire in the tundra."

"Yes," I say.

"But every day, in every letter, you tell little kids that you talked to Santa himself. And that's not true, Francie. You tell a huge, mountainous, snow-covered Santa Claus lie," she says.

There are a million better responses than the one I offer.

I could tell Alice that it is not the same thing. That God and church are different.

I could tell her that none of it matters. That we are friends anyway. And that we'll get to spend more time together once Dad shows Aunt Carole who is boss and I pass probation and earn enough money to buy the Miata.

I could tell her that I'm doing what I can do.

But what I say is this: Santa is not a lie.

37

It takes about an hour and a half for ten minutes to pass. When DeKieser finally texts Alice, she and I sneak out of the linen closet and down to the playroom where we find Hector and DeKieser and a handful of not-in-hospital-gown kids hovering around a Christmas tree. Hector has his gown flap toward the wall.

"Do you have my pants?" he asks. Alice holds up the Santa bag, but he doesn't take it from her. He needs his hands to hold his flap shut. "Santa just left. It sounded like he is going to visit a kid in her room."

"Did you record my Aunt Carole?"

DeKieser shrugs. "She didn't say much," says DeKieser. "She and all these people in suits just stood around and, like, watched and stuff."

"Of course," I say. I must sound angry because Hector looks wary.

"I know you were worried about him," he says, "but the Santa guy seemed really good. The kids were happy. The parents were crying. Your aunt and all the businesspeople had goofy looks on their faces."

"Oh, I'm sure," I say. "I've seen the act." It's just what Aunt Carole would want. Slick. Phony. Putting on a big show for the business types. Of course he is. And of course Hector can't tell. "You never saw my Grampa Chris," I tell him. "You never saw the real Santa in action. You never—" I say and then I remember that this isn't over. Santa has not left the building. Right now he is probably using some poor dying child to audition for the suits of Hollydale while Aunt Carole snaps photos for marketing brochures.

Well, not if I can help it. I fling open the playroom doors and thunder around the corner, narrowly missing a gurney and an empty wheelchair.

"Francie!" I hear Alice whisper-call behind me. I spin around but keep walking backward. Hector and DeKieser are following Alice, all of them looking like I'm some rabid Old Yeller they need to stop before he reaches town.

"Francie, like—" DeKieser points and I spin around again, just in time to prevent a backward collision with Aunt Carole. Instead I hit her head on.

Aunt Carole is a tall woman, which is the only thing that saves me from discovering whether she shares the family bloody nose gene. Aunt Carole's chin shatters—or maybe it's my skull? The hospital hallway dims and tilts.

"Catch her!" someone says. There are arms around me. The hallway rights itself. Four Aunt Caroles scowl at me. Then three, then two, then one.

"Are you crying?" I ask her.

"I am in pain, Frances. You hit me."

"I didn't hit you, I bumped into you. I was coming to stop—"

"Shhhhhh," says a voice near my ear. It belongs to the arms that are still around me. Hector, I think. Hector has his arms around me. Hector is supporting me. Which is good because the thought makes me dizzy all over again.

"Are you okay?" Alice slides into view. So does DeKieser. So does Hector. Hector is magical, I decide. He can stand in front of me looking so concerned at the same time he's got me in his arms.

"Shhh," says the ear voice again. I'm lifted to balance on my own two feet. The arms that have been holding me do not belong to Hector. They belong to a man in a fedora. He is wearing a hospital mask over half his face, but his eyes look familiar. Sparkly. The kind that see you when you're sleeping.

"Santa Slick?" I ask.

"Shhhh," he says again, and he steps a little closer to the doorway we've stopped in front of. He is eavesdropping and he waves me over to do the same.

Just beyond the door a small voice says, "I've been good."

"You've been very good." A deeper voice. Bigger. But not loud, not overwhelming. Just wide, maybe, like it could wrap itself around you if you needed.

"My mom has been good too."

"She takes good care of you," says the deep, wide voice. "She loves you a lot, doesn't she?"

"She wants me to get better for Christmas. She wants me to be all better."

It is quiet. It is so quiet.

"I don't think I'm going to get better by Christmas," the little voice continues. "You can't make me better either, can you?"

"No, honey, I can't. There are some things even Santa can't do."

In my mind I see Grampa Chris. I see him take the small leather book from his pocket. I see the tiny silver pencil.

"You look tired, sweetheart. Is there anything Santa can do for you? Do you want to rest?"

I am tired, I think.

"When my mom is here," says the little voice, "she holds my hand until I fall asleep."

"She is a very good mom, isn't she?" The wide voice chuckles. Not in a funny way or a showy way. Just the way that says he is listening. That you are worth his time. Worth his love. "Would you like me to hold your hand?"

Yes, I think.

"You'll stay until I fall asleep?" asks the girl.

"Of course I will," says Santa. "You rest. You rest, now. Santa will be here as long as you need him."

Santa Slick has stepped away. Aunt Carole too. But Alice is there beside me. She sniffs. Wipes her nose on her sleeve. "Fine," she whispers. "Fine."

I know exactly what she means.

Aunt Carole and Santa Slick have found some chairs a little way down the hall. Hector and DeKieser stand beside them. As we get closer, I can hear Santa Slick explaining his mask to DeKieser. "Covers the beard," he says. "We don't want to confuse the children by having two Santas in the room."

Two Santas. I must still be a little dizzy from my collision with Aunt Carole because I'm just now realizing that if Brady McCaffery, Celebrity Santa, is here in the hallway, then he cannot also have been the Santa in that hospital room.

"Who was that?" I ask. "Talking with that little girl? Who did the party?"

"A very good man," says Brady McCaffery. "Carole, you were right. I am glad I came to see one of your students in action. You and your school should be proud."

"Imagine how much better it would be if—" Aunt Carole starts, but Brady McCaffery isn't listening. He is looking past me, down the hallway to where the warm-voiced

Santa is now standing, silent, with his back to the room he has just left. I recognize him instantly.

"Santa Franklin," I say.

"Excuse me," says Mr. McCaffery. He approaches Santa Franklin with an arm extended, like he is going to shake his hand, but ends up with his hand on the man's shoulder. They stand there together. If they speak, I don't hear it.

What I do hear is the buzzing of a cell phone. DeKieser's. "My mom is in the parking lot. I told her to, like, pick me up here. Are you going to be okay?" she asks me.

She's asking about the bump on my forehead from my mid-aunt collision. I just caught a glimpse of it in a fire extinguisher window. It's ruby red and as round as Rudolph's nose.

"I'll be okay," I say at the same time Alice asks if maybe DeKieser could give her a ride home too?

"Francie," she explains, "I've got something—"

She doesn't need to finish. She's got a story to write for the *Daily*, I know.

"Go," I say. What else can I say? Sacrifice your writing dreams so you can stand here with me as I try to figure out all the ways I've been an idiot?

Aunt Carole wasn't sabotaging the school at all—she was showing it off. Although, she *was* sneaking behind my dad's back and showing it off to the guy she hopes to stage a Santa School coup with, which is still pretty rotten. Though maybe not so pressingly rotten as to justify truck theft?

Rattling bracelets bring me back to my senses. Before Aunt Carole can ask me what I'm doing here—or, worse, how I got here in the first place—I tell her I have to go too.

"Hector has work," I say. "I have . . . I'll see you at the shop." I grab Hector's arm and pull him toward the elevator bank. "Let's get out of here," I whisper.

"Okay," he whispers back. "But where are my pants?"

We ride the elevator for a bit while I try to reach Alice. It takes me three tries to text **Do you have the Santa bag?** (First two attempts: **Do you hate the Satan ban?** and **Dojo have the Santa badger?**) She does not reply to any of them.

Occasionally, people ride the elevator with us. Some have snow in their hair and on their shoulders. I guess the weatherman wasn't kidding.

"I can't go out in a snowstorm without pants," says Hector.

"I'd give you mine but I don't think they'd fit."

"Really?" he says. Not like he wants to try on my pants, but like it means a lot that I would offer. After everything I asked him to do for me today, Hector Ramirez is grateful for my empty gesture. He's a good person, Hector Ramirez is, and for the hundredth time since alcohol-free teen night at the Torino I wish I had had faith. I wish I had not run away. I wish I had let him kiss me. If, in fact, he actually wanted to kiss me.

Of course I don't actually say any of that. What I do say is, "Maybe we could swap coats."

His leather jacket is big on me and my sleeping bag coat barely fits over Hector's mighty fine shoulders, but it is long enough to reach his knees. I can tell by his face that he's not a fan of the look, but he doesn't say anything except, "Let's go."

Luckily Hector left his wallet and the keys to Uncle Jack's truck in the pocket of his jacket, not his pants. I hand them back to him as we run through the parking lot snow. The wind is whipping around and the flakes are fat and wet. Most of them melt as they hit the pavement, but we've been in the hospital long enough that we have to brush a thin layer of white from the truck's windshield.

Hector puts the keys in the ignition. He checks his mirrors. He checks them again. He turns up the heat. He checks his mirrors a third time then backs slowly, excruciatingly slowly, out of the parking space.

"I've never driven in snow," he says.

"Have faith," I tell him. "And turn on your headlights."

Hector pushes a button and Willie Nelson warbles "Jingle Bells" at us.

"Radio," says Hector.

"Radio," I say.

Hector pushes a few more buttons until, finally, the headlights shine a stark, blue-white glow into the flurries. The ground in front of us glistens.

"Headlights," Hector says.

"Yes," I confirm.

Hector puts the truck into drive and inches forward.

He speeds up, then slows down again. "Just testing the brakes."

I nod supportively as the interior cab light dims and Hector, hands at nine and three, presses gently on the accelerator.

38

For the next thirty minutes, Hector seems torn between the twin impulses to proceed with extreme caution and to end this drive as soon as possible. The sky grows darker. Hector takes his foot off the gas every time another car approaches and doesn't put it back on until it passes. Sometimes I catch him glancing at me, as if he's embarrassed, but I pretend to be fascinated by the wipers clunking back and forth on the windshield.

Snow-*clunk*-no snow-*clunk*.

Snow-*clunk*-no snow-*clunk*.

Like one of Ms. Colando's myth oppositions.

Which has me thinking about oppositions in general. Can a person believe that two opposing things are equally true? If I were smarter or less stress-avoiding could I accept, as Alice does, Catholic school while also rejecting some of the things it teaches? There are so many things about the mythologies of Christmas that I've questioned— the economic inequalities, the way it can overshadow other religious traditions, the commercialism that our family shop depends on—but at the same time I am 100% certain about the Santa moment that Grampa Chris believed in. That moment when a child turns to Santa and is listened to and loved.

This is the part, I've been thinking, that Aunt Carole doesn't understand about Santa and the school and Grampa Chris—but even as I think that, I remember what I read in Bryan's notebook and feel a tiny twinge of sympathy. She felt pushed out of the family business. How awful must that have been? I mean, it doesn't change the fact that she made me wear humiliating outfits or that she tried to ruin *An Evening with Santa* or that there are hundreds of unanswered letters to Santa's Intern sitting in Snowflake right now, but still, how hard must it have been to know your dad was there listening—truly listening—to the wishes of every kid in Hollydale . . . except yours?

"Jingle Bells" is still on the radio, but now it is being half-sung/half-spoken by someone who sounds a lot like Captain Kirk. It seems we are tuned in to a "Jingle Bells" marathon and I just now realize that we've heard at least five other versions of this song, including ones by Gwen Stefani, Pearl Jam, and a Muppet.

As far as I can tell, Hector hasn't noticed the Jingle Bellery either. He's focused. Quiet. Driving in the almost complete dark. I can no longer see him, really, but I know that there in the driver's seat is a boy with fine shoulders and constellation skin and soft brown eyes and lips I regret very much not kissing. I can't see them, but I know these things are there. There's a logic in that, of course. It is rational to believe in the persistence of these physical things. What defies logic, however, what tests faith, is his belief in *me*. His and DeKieser's and even Alice's. They put their faith in me. They added their faith to the Intern letters. They helped me spy on Aunt Carole. Hector—this sweet, cautious, nervous-as-anything Hector—is actually half dressed and breaking the law, taking real risks because he believed in *me*.

Hector slows down again and hits the turn signal, even though our first turning opportunity is still a quarter mile away.

"You doing okay?" I ask.

I feel him startle a little. "Me? Oh . . . sure," he says. "I'm fine." He presses the gas then and the truck rumbles to a speed just a little over the limit as he reaches the turn. Behind us, something large and heavy slides from one side of the truck bed to the other, landing with a hollow *whump*.

Hector takes his foot of the gas. The thing under the tarp slides again. *Szszszzzzzzzzzzz . . . whump!*

"What was that?" Hector asks. I can't see his eyes in the dark, but I'm certain they are wide.

"I'm not sure."

"Should we stop?" asks Hector.

It would probably be good to stop, but I can't imagine where. It seems dangerous to just pull over on the side of the road. We're almost to the shop anyway, and the longer this ride takes, the greater the possibility that Aunt Carole will beat us home and catch me in this less-than-authorized use of Uncle Jack's truck. "Keep going," I tell him. "There's a tarp over the back. It's not like something's going to fly out."

Hector nods and pushes the gas pedal. The thing in the truck bed slides again. *Szszszzzzzzz . . . whump.*

Captain Kirk's song/speech ends and Barbra Streisand takes over the jingling. We play this one at the store sometimes. The song is fast and breathless and every time I hear it I am reminded of one of my least favorite student-elves, a man who called himself Tinsel and would not stop juggling tiny expensive ornaments. I'm about to snap off the radio when I notice that Hector is nervously singing along.

I think Hector notices me noticing him, because he stops singing for a second. Also, the truck slows down.

He cannot slow down. "Keep going," I say.

Hector speeds up. He also starts singing again, this time a little louder. Behind us, the thing in the trunk slides. *Szszszzzzzz . . .* but before the *whump* comes I join in the singing, hoping to drown it out a little.

Jinglebellsjinglebells/ING-GLE BELLS!
Jinglebellsjinglebells/ANG-GLE BELLS!

By the time we get to the big open-sleigh finish, Hector is driving the speed limit and we are both singing at top volume. The snow is falling in fat, wet flakes as he speeds up to beat the light at Fair and Main. The thing in the truck bed *whumps* the tailgate again.

We're nearly home. I can see the North Pole and the library tree lot across the street. It looks beautiful with the lights strung up above it and families bunched up around their trees of choice. For a second the world seems snowy and sweet and perfect and I find myself thinking again about Christmas miracles when, in an instant, everything changes. A quarter mile ahead of us, on the opposite side of the median, an SUV slides, then spins a full turn and three-quarters, its high beams filling the cab of the truck not once, but twice before stopping perpendicular to the road, its front wheels bouncing up onto the curb, headlights aimed perfectly at Aunt Carole's enormous disco wreath.

Before Hector can react, the windshield is pierced by a thousand blinding pinpricks of light. Instinctively I close my eyes. Hector, I suspect, does the same while simultaneously slamming his foot hard on the breaks. Uncle Jack's truck skids and slides, swerving into the right lane and then back again before smacking hard against the curb. *Whomp* goes the car. *WHUMP!* goes the thing under the tarp. I open my eyes just in time to see Rudolph the

Red-Nosed Reindeer soaring over the cab of Uncle Jack's truck. For a moment, it looks as if he'll just keep flying up and away into the dark Hollydale night, but then gravity takes hold, and Rudolph plummets, red-nose–first, into the median ditch.

It takes a moment before I am able to open the truck door and step outside. Hector follows, stunned. We stand unmoving in the whipping winter wind, fat flakes swirling among the dancing disco lights, and take in the holiday carnage. In the cab of the truck, Streisand gives way to barking dogs.

Finally, Hector breaks the silence. "Now what?" he asks.

As if in answer to his question, headlights appear behind us. A car door creaks open and shuts. I turn to see a backlit figure moving closer, plump and booted and coming to our rescue.

Could it be?

Hector says what I am thinking. "Santa?"

For a moment, I feel a ridiculously wonderful relief. Santa will fix this. Santa can fix anything, I think, even as I hear my grandfather's words again. *Santa is magic, but he does not do magic. There's only so much you can do.* Even Santa can't magically heal a mechanical reindeer. And besides, my brain tells me, finally catching up, this can't be the one true Santa because there is no one true Santa. There are only Santas. There is only Santa magic.

And as if to prove that, the person in the boots becomes

visible. It is not even a guy in a Santa suit. It is Uncle Jack. So long, Miata. It was nice dreaming about you.

"Good evening, Francie," Uncle Jack says when he reaches the truck. "Who's your friend?"

"This is Hector Ramirez," I say.

"Sir." Hector reaches out to shake Uncle Jack's hand, but Uncle Jack is studying the hospital gown that Hector is still wearing under my coat, likely trying to figure out whether this is some trendy high school fashion statement or if Hector is contagious. Uncle Jack seems not to want to take chances and instead lumbers over to squat ditch-side. He peers down into the hollow.

Hector squats beside him. "Is he going to be all right?" Hector asks. Uncle Jack regards him in a way that tells me he has made up his mind about the hospital garb.

"You understand it's a mechanical deer, don't you, son?"

Hector looks at me.

"I'm sorry, Uncle Jack. We were at the hospital. . . ." I don't know where to start. With Santa Slick in the children's ward? With Aunt Carole's plans to take over the business? With Dad being so tired and needing help?

Uncle Jack tilts his head toward Hector. "Francie, is this boy okay?" He lowers his voice, though not enough that Hector can't hear him. "Does he need medication?"

Hector bugs his eyes at me.

"He's fine," I say. "He doesn't need anything."

"He needs pants," says Uncle Jack.

"Pants would be nice," says Hector. "Sir."

"There's a pair of overalls under the back seat of the cab." He pats Hector on the shoulder, then points at the truck. "Go on, son. Get some britches on. Then come back here and help Francie and me take care of Rudolph."

Once Rudolph is in the truck bed Uncle Jack orders us into the cab, drives us up Santa Claus Lane, and parks in the five-bay garage.

"I'm sorry," I say, but Uncle Jack stops me.

"I'm going to fetch the Miata now. I'll be right back." He slides out of the truck, pockets the keys, and shuts the door. It doesn't take long for the heat to leave the cab.

"Want to switch back?" asks Hector. "Coats?"

Of course. I am still wearing his coat. And he is wearing mine. And he probably wants to bail. Who wouldn't?

We switch coats. I try not to notice that my coat now smells like pine needles. I worry that his jacket now smells like failure.

He zips up his jacket. Jams his hands in the pockets.

"You can go," I tell him. "You can go to the tree lot and find Luis if you want. I'll explain everything to Uncle Jack."

Hector checks his watch. "My shift doesn't start for another twenty minutes. I'll wait with you. You know. . . if you don't mind."

I don't mind. I don't mind a bit. But I don't say that

because I don't know what to say. *I'm sorry I got you into this mess? I'm sorry I misunderstood my aunt's plans? I'm sorry I didn't kiss you when I had the chance?* "I'm sorry," I start, but I chicken out. "That, um . . . that I missed your presentation. In class. I mean, I was there, but—"

"You fell asleep. I know."

"You know? You could tell?"

"You were drooling, Francie."

I was drooling. Great. "I'm sorry," I say again.

"I've been thinking . . . ," Hector says, and I wait for him to tell me that he's changed his mind. That he's going to head over to the tree lot anyway. That he'll see me in school sometime. But that is not what he says.

"I've been thinking how hard it must be to pretend you know everything" is what he says.

Pretend what? I don't—

"I've been thinking about that Santa at the hospital and about what you said about Santas needing to know history and geography. But it's a lot, right? I mean, the guys at your school *aren't* Santa. They're just people. And there's a lot of ways for people to mess up. I mean, what about languages? Is Santa supposed to know every language? What if a kid is visiting from China? Does Santa speak Mandarin?"

He isn't the first to ask this question, of course. I asked Grampa Chris this question myself once, when one of Alice's cousins was visiting from Seoul. He admitted it was a hard one. Most of the time, he told me, there is an auntie or a cousin around who speaks English and can signal whether Santa should nod or shake his head. And mostly, a Santa's job is to listen. Still, I tell Hector, a good Santa should be able to say a few things in at least a couple of languages. *Merry Christmas. I'm glad to see you. What would you like Santa to know?* "They can't really have a full-on conversation," I say, "but—"

"But it's something," he says. "It shows they care."

I nod, because it is true. "And I guess if you have to choose, caring is a lot more important than perfection."

Hector smiles. "It's certainly easier to believe in."

Hector Ramirez is a remarkable human being. I know this to be true, though I can no longer claim any kind of objectivity about the matter. And I know, too, that he is letting me off the hook for everything. For losing his pants and being traumatized by a reindeer and sitting here in a dark, cold truck. It's all okay, he's saying. But I need to apologize anyway.

"I am sorry," I tell him again, "about everything. I'm sorry. . . ." I'm sure I sound pathetic, like I'm just trying to get myself out of trouble, and I don't want him to think that. "How do you say 'I'm sorry' in Spanish?" I ask.

"'I'm sorry?'" asks Hector. "Uh . . . that would be 'lo siento.'"

"Lo siento," I tell him. "And how do you say 'I'm an idiot'?" I ask.

Hector laughs. "'Soy idiota.' Except you're not an idiot,

Francie. You're a girl who cares about her family and about kids and . . . stuff matters to you. I like that things matter." He stops talking and looks at me. He has very nice eyes, Hector Ramirez does. And lips. Which is probably why I ask what I ask next.

"How do you say 'I'm fully vaccinated'?"

A look of confusion comes over Hector's face. "What? Um. 'Tengo todas mis vacunas.'"

"And how about 'I like you and with your permission, I would really like to kiss you'?"

"'Me gustas,'" says Hector. He is quieter than he was before, and yet his voice is all that I can hear. "'Me gustas mucho y con tu permiso—'"

He doesn't finish his sentence. He can't. Because my mouth is on his. Because I am kissing him.

It's an eight at least. Maybe higher. Maybe . . . "Was that okay?" I ask.

"Ah, sí, muy bueno," says Hector.

I don't have to know Spanish to understand that this is a good thing. "Muy bueno," I say. My accent is not exactly right, and I want to try again, but Hector stops me.

"Francie—" Hector starts, and just like that I am underwater, holding my breath, scrambling for something to say, something in any language. "I think we can do better," he says. And then his lips are soft on mine and his fingers slide up along my neck and into my hair and Hector Ramirez kisses me, really kisses me, and the world dissolves like snow on breath. The kiss is long and sweet and tender. It is a kiss with hope in it, with possibility. It is a kiss of consequence.

Also? Objectively?

A ten.

39

By the time Uncle Jack returns with the Miata, Hector and I have achieved several tens. My lips are tingly and warm, although my fingers and the rest of me are frozen.

If Uncle Jack can tell about the lips, he doesn't say so, but he can see how cold we are. "Let's go to the Pole and get you kids some coffee," he says to me. "Might be able to scrounge up a school sweatshirt for your friend, too. Be warmer than the dress he's got on under those overalls."

I want to tell him Hector isn't wearing a dress, but as soon as I start talking, I figure, I'm going to have to explain everything, including how I thought it was a good idea to borrow his truck for the afternoon.

We make our way across the parking lot without talking, Johnny Mathis desperate to convince us that winter is a marshmallow world. The ice pellets bouncing off my face do not feel like marshmallows. Then Hector reaches for my hand. "Okay?" he asks me.

I nod. Ice pellets? What ice pellets?

The North Pole kitchen is warm. Two seasonal employees from Ornaments are at the table eating snickerdoodles. "I don't know how we're going to get it all on the floor on time," says one.

"Eh, you do what you can do," says the other.

I hear my Grampa Chris again. See that small leather book. The tiny silver pencil.

In the next room, in Snowflake, are five boxes of letters to Santa's Intern. Letters asking for toys. Letters asking for clothes. Letters just to tell me I'm doing a good job and please say hello to Santa from Ollie. From Marisol. From Lana. From Kim. Every one of those kids deserves a response. Every one deserves to know that Santa cares. That he has listened. That he will be there for them as long as they need. I'm going to answer those letters. I won't be able to get to most of them before Christmas, but I'm going to do what I can do. And I'm going to start now.

"Hey, Uncle Jack, Hector—if it's okay with you, I have some stuff I have to do. Can we—Uncle Jack—can we talk about all this stuff tomorrow? I promise I'll explain everything."

Uncle Jack gives me as stern a look as he can, which isn't very stern at all. He just doesn't have it in him. "We'll talk tomorrow. But before you take off to do whatever it is you have to do, let's get this boy dressed."

"I'm okay," says Hector. But Uncle Jack is right. Although he has borrowed Uncle Jack's overalls, that hospital gown can't be warm and Hector has to go work outside in the Christmas lot in a few minutes.

"No, come on," I say, waving him toward Snowflake. "Let's find you a Santa School commemorative sweatshirt. It's the least I can do to say thanks."

I open the door to Snowflake. Then close it again.

"What's the matter?" asks Uncle Jack.

"There is a puckhe—" I stop myself. "I think there is a hockey player in Snowflake."

"Are you sure?" asks Hector.

It does seem strange. And I did bump my head pretty hard. I open the door again and peek inside. I was wrong. There is not a hockey player in Snowflake. There are five hockey players sitting at the huge conference table in Snowflake. One of them sticks out his tongue. Someone else smacks him in the head.

"I said we weren't doing that anymore," says the smacker. It is Gunther Hobbes, star forward, *BEER* drinker, brother of Gordie, and now . . . what? "Hi, Francie," he says to me.

"Hi, Francie," say the rest of the puckheads. They are joined by several members of the Hollydale High School student body that I recognize by clique if not by name. A theater kid and a few of the comics girls from Mythology Today. The Dobler, Anthony, is here, too, holding hands with Ellie, who is rushing—fake breathless—up to greet me.

"'Mary did it, George! Mary did it!'" she shouts. "'She told a few people you were in trouble and they scattered all over town.'"

"*It's a Wonderful Life*," says Anthony, explaining the reference. He beams with pride.

"Actually, Alice did it," says DeKieser. She and Alice are there, too. They have moved the boxes of letters to the floor in front of the fireplace and are standing proudly before them. "She went through my phone and, like, called a bunch of people and here we are."

I glance at Hector, who seems as lost as I am. "Here for what?" I ask.

"Emergency interns to Santa's Intern reporting for duty," says Gunther. "Hey guys, scoot over, there's more people here to help." He slaps the tongue kid again, then points to the door behind us. "Give that guy a pen."

The slapee pops up with a fistful of felt-tip pens and holds them out to the new helpers, who are not really new helpers at all. They are my mom and dad, just back from Chicago, and—now appearing in the doorway just behind them—Aunt Carole and Santa Slick.

Oh, holy night.

"Francie," says Dad. "What are all these people doing here?"

"I . . . I'm not entirely sure?" I say.

Alice springs into action. "Earlier today," she explains,

with only the slightest Miss Fisherian clip, "Francie learned that there were actually a lot more Intern letters to write than she had been led to believe." She pauses to send a cutting look Aunt Carole's way before continuing. "Thus, we're all pitching in to help."

"You are?" I say. "What about your news story?"

"Submitted," she says.

"And hockey practice?" I ask Gunther. "You guys are always on the ice."

"Community skate day," says Gunther. "Besides, I didn't want any of those elf assassins coming after me if I said no."

"Elf assassins?" asks Dad.

"Nobody wanted these kids not to get a letter back from Santa," says a comics girl.

"From Santa's Intern," corrects another.

They are here to write letters. All of them. They have pens and Intern stationery and small stacks of envelopes with kid printing on them.

Dad shakes his head. "That's very nice of you all," he says, "but I'm afraid I'm going to have to send you home. I told Francie"—he turns to look at me directly—"Francie, I told you that *you* were the only one who could answer these letters. If you needed help you should have come to me. These kids aren't trained. They don't know anything about Santa or the responsibility we have."

"Francie trained me," says Gunther.

"I did?" I must have hit my head harder than I thought.

"At your store. You said Santa doesn't make promises."

"Well, I guess I did—"

"Never use a name unless you're one hundred percent sure you've got it right," says a theater kid.

"Be kind, be personal," says Ellie.

"Repeat the kid's wishes in case the parent doesn't know yet," says Anthony.

"Show them Santa is listening," says Hector. "That's all we can really give anyone in the end—our attention and our love."

Even though Hector is talking about the kids of Hollydale and surrounding areas, and even though we have only just kissed and that is in no way a profession of anything even approaching love, I believe I blush a distinctly crimson blush. It is possible that Hector does too.

Dad is not blushing. He is still looking a little angry, though it is possible he has softened.

"Mr. Wood," says Alice, "we haven't sealed a single envelope. Francie has to approve every word before a single letter goes out."

"Those are the letters you've written?" asks Mom. She is looking at the boxes in front of the Snowflake hearth.

"Those are the letters that just came in," says Alice. She looks accusingly at Carole again. "All six hundred and forty-one of them."

"That is a lot of letters," says Mom. "And Christmas is just a week away."

"Precisely," says Alice.

"Even if each emergency intern writes what seems like an optimistic average of thirty letters, Francie will still have more than one hundred fifty replies to write before Monday afternoon in order to get all of them to the post office by five so they will arrive at their destinations by Christmas Eve," says DeKieser. "I've, like, done the math."

From the doorway I hear the rattle of bracelets and an intake of breath as Aunt Carole prepares to weigh in, but before she can say a single word, Santa Slick says seven.

"Well, then," he says. "We'd better get to work."

"Brady," says Aunt Carole. "You don't have to—"

"Of course, I do," he says. The sees-you-when-you're-sleeping look is on his face. "We don't want to be the ones to sow the seed of doubt."

"My father used to say that all the time," Dad says.

Santa Slick smiles. "I read it in your manual. Carole sent it to me. Your father ran a beautiful school, Mr. Wood. You're right to be proud of it." He takes a pen and makes his way to the conference table. "Can you show me what to do?" he asks Gunther.

Gunther Hobbes, star forward, fashion expert, brother of Gordie, slapper of heads, actually beams. "Move it," he tells a puckhead. "Make room for Santa Claus."

"There's room for you too, Carole." Santa Slick holds up a pen. Aunt Carole is still standing in the doorway. She doesn't move. She looks like I did in Ellie's movie, framed by the Tree Shed doors. Small. Alone. Outside.

I could tell Dad that this is all her fault right now if I

wanted to. I could tell him that she hid the letters from me and tried to sabotage the school. But I don't. Instead I take the pen from Santa Slick and walk it over to her. "Come on," I say quietly, so no one else can hear. "It's the closest most of us will ever get to being Santa Claus."

Aunt Carole takes the pen.

"Nick, get a pen and take a seat," says Mom. "I'm going to print more stationery."

Dad obeys. It's a little tight around the table, but nothing like when we have thirty-five Santa students in here. I hand Dad a small stack of letters. "We're going to have a serious talk tomorrow," he tells me.

I'll pencil you in after Uncle Jack, I want to say, but even with a low-grade head injury I have better judgment than that. "Okay" is what I tell hm.

"Francie," Hector whispers. "I'm sorry. I want to help, but I just texted Luis and the tree lot is really busy."

"It's okay. Go. Your work is important too," I say.

His eyes meet mine. They are remarkable eyes. Warm and soft, and if it weren't for his outstanding lips I would say they are my favorite part of his face, but after our time in the cab of Uncle Jack's truck, I'll have to call that a draw. Hector's eyes say he wants to kiss me now. He wants to kiss me right here in Snowflake in front of everyone. I'd like to kiss him too, I think. Maybe. But not in front of everyone. Not when it might look like I'm trying to prove something. He must be able to tell that too, because the kissing *right now* look fades into an *okay, not now, but soon* look. Like I said, they are remarkable eyes.

I find him a sweatshirt and, once I spy the Santa bag under Alice's chair, hand him that too. "You're going to be late," I tell him. "You can bring back the bag and Uncle Jack's stuff another time."

"Yeah?" He says it hopefully, like I have just asked him on a date.

"Sure," I say. "Yes," I say. "Please." Which probably sounds the same way.

When Hector leaves, Alice gathers up some of the replies that have already been written and hands them to me to read. The room goes quiet. Everyone—Dad, Aunt Carole, Uncle Jack, Santa Brady, the hockey dudes, the film kids, the comics girls, Ellie, Anthony, Alice, DeKieser—everyone is opening letters. They are reading. They are writing. They are doing what they can do.

> *Dear Jenny*
> *Dear Martine*
> *Dear Tyrell*
> *Dear Janaiya*
> *Dear Kiddo*
> *Dear Friend*

They do a good job, the emergency interns. We don't get any difficult letters like Olivia's or the kind Grampa Chris would have penciled in his notebook, but a few responses need extra care and one of the hockey guys—Miller is his name—hands off some of the trickiest letters to more confident writers.

Aunt Carole gets one of them. A kid who wants to be a great basketball player but hasn't scored a single basket all season.

> *Dear Julia:*
> *Santa knows how hard it is when you want to be able to do something and you can't yet—he says you should have seen him try to fly the sleigh the first time! But Santa kept at it and now he's a pro. You'd be surprised at how much you can grow if you're willing. Keep practicing, Julia. I'll be rooting for you.*

"That's really good," I tell Aunt Carole.

"I am aware of that," she says.

It takes nearly four and a half hours for almost every Intern letter to be opened and read and replied to. I have not been able to approve all the responses yet, but I don't have to work until tomorrow afternoon and Dad says that in the morning, after church, he and I can read through the rest together. After we have our talk.

"Okay," I say, just as my phone buzzes. It is Hector.

How did it go? he texts.

I respond slowly and carefully. O, I type. K.

I have to work a lot this week.

Me too, I say. So far so good.

And I have a lot of homework. And there's hockey.

Is he trying to get out of seeing me? Is he filled with regret? Was I wrong about the tens?

But I'd like to return the Santa bag, says Hector. And, you know.

I do know. And I was not wrong about the tens. I steady my thumbs and type my reply.

What are you doing X-men Eve?

40

It is a Holiday Shop tradition to close the store at four so employees can go home and begin Christmas with their families. Most do go home, but the old-timers like Dottie and Jerry and the people without nearby families stay for our annual holiday party, which is held half indoors, half outdoors, with a bonfire in the fire pit in Outdoor Decor and the barn doors of the Tree Shed flung open wide.

This year, Dad has invited the emergency interns as well. Most couldn't come but Alice is here, of course. And Ellie and her Dobler. DeKieser and her girlfriend, Kelsey. Gunther brought a couple of the hockey guys and his little sister, Gordie, with him. "When Spinek heard about the party he said he was going to stop by," Gunther says, "but I told him he probably shouldn't."

"You said he if showed up, elf assassins would slap shot him," says Gordie.

"Something like that," says Gunther.

Alice and I watch Gordie drag her brother to the line to see Santa Claus. He looks sweet, Gunther does, holding his sister's hand. So sweet it is hard to imagine him slap shotting anyone, though when I picture such a thing happening to Sam Spinek I have to admit a certain satisfaction.

"You okay with this?" asks Alice. She sees me looking at the Santa line and, I suspect, is really asking if I'm okay with the Santa at the head of it. For the first time since Grampa Chris died, my dad is not suited up for Christmas Eve. Santa Franklin is.

"Yeah, I'm okay," I tell Alice. "Dad needs a break. It's been a hard year."

He told me so himself on Sunday when I met him in Snowflake for our "talk."

It was my second talk of the day. Already that morning I had apologized to Uncle Jack, who had gone easy on me, of course, forgiving me before I could even say *I'm sorry*— though he did make me promise to let him teach me to drive. "That way, if you get any more dumbbell ideas, you won't get your friends in trouble too." Agreeing to his plan was easy, especially after he explained that his old truck was actually somewhat finicky to drive and that we'd be using the Miata for lessons instead.

Talking with Dad was harder. I had a lot of explaining and apologizing to do. He did some explaining too. It seems, he told me, that Bryan's notebook had gone missing. She had assured him that she didn't need it anymore—her college semester was over—but its absence meant there was no complete record of my Pillar Points. Without the notebook, Dad would have to trust me that things had gone well and give me a raise. Or, he let me know, he could trust Aunt Carole that the opposite had been true and that I should be laid off until I had matured a little.

So which was it? Had I been naughty or had I been nice?

As it turns out, Dad's thinking is a little more complicated than the simple naughty/nice opposition. I would not get a raise, nor would I be fired. Instead, Dad informed me with a not-quite-Clausian twinkle in his eye, that once the holiday season was over, I would continue to receive minimum wage for another ninety days but would be transferred to a new position. I would be an intern. Aunt Carole's intern.

As you might imagine, my protests had little effect, and in truth, did not go on for long. Aunt Carole, Dad explained, wanted to make some changes in the way we run Santa School and he didn't have the time to oversee both the shop and her machinations. "I need someone who cares about its traditions to help her," he said.

My suggestion that Aunt Carole be *my* intern did not, apparently, warrant consideration. But I was to consider this: that Dad had decided to let Aunt Carole invite Santa Slick—I mean, Santa Brady—to be a guest speaker at the school next year. It would be a trial sort of thing. I would be keeping notes and doing a complete evaluation. I've already picked out a notebook. I've also already made two notes about things to discuss with Aunt Carole, two things that even *I* think are worth changing: (1) Santa training should be open to everyone, not just men. (2) No one, regardless of age, class, race, or gender, should be encouraged to elf.

Okay, I said. Is that it?

That was it from Christopher Wood, my boss. But Christopher Wood, my father, had three things to add:

(1) He was extraordinarily proud of me yesterday, and watching me coach emergency interns had been one of the highlights of his life as a parent.

(2) Regardless of the fact that Uncle Jack had forgiven me for "borrowing" his truck, Dad had not, and he wanted me to know that if I ever, ever, ever did a thing like that again I could forget getting my driver's license until I was eighteen.

(3) In the name of restorative justice, I would be responsible for Rudolph repairs, a rough estimate for which he just happened to have on hand.

And so it is that as I stand here watching Gordie Hobbes climb into the lap of Santa Franklin, on this, the night before Christmas, after working hard all holiday season, I am four dollars poorer than I was at its start. Any annoying bright side–seeing elf would also point out that my friendship with Alice is tighter than ever, it's been a week since anyone other than my brothers has stuck out their tongues at me, and I've made several new friends—including a star forward hockey player. I'm on my way to learning how to drive, and wonder of wonders, I have had and continue to have kisses of consequence with a fine-shouldered, voice-over-voiced, constellation-skinned, kindhearted, tender-lipped, remarkable-eyed boy. A boy who has just now left his LumberJuan charity tree lot gig to join me and Alice here in front of the Christmas Eve bonfire for a chorus of "O Tannenbaum." The scent of pine is swoon worthy. Or maybe that's just Hector.

All around there are carolers and cocoa and kids—lots of kids—laughing and squealing and chasing one another through Outdoor Decor.

"Marla," I hear someone yell, "you stay away from that manger. The baby Jesus is not a toy!"

My parents are holding hands and DeKieser is helping Gram hand out bags of caramel corn, and although there is no mistletoe minefield near Snowman Alley, Ellie and her Dobler don't seem to know it. Aunt Carole is sitting by the bonfire with Uncle Jack, and while I'm not entirely sure that she is having a good time, I'm not sure that she isn't either. It's not exactly a Christmas miracle, but it's something.

Alice and Hector and I watch a mob of preschoolers follow Don and Dash past the cookie table and into the Tree Shed. It is beautiful, the Tree Shed. The overhead lights are dimmed and the trees are shining and the tiny fairy lights that line the path are golden and warm.

"Big difference between your trees and the ones I worked with all season," says Hector.

"Are you calling our trees fake?"

"Fake? Look at that kid." Hector points to a tiny boy, no older than four. He's got a stripey hat on and a bright orange coat. One of his pantlegs is tucked into his boot and the other isn't, but the kid doesn't care. His mouth is open, his eyes shine. He's standing just inside the Tree Shed doors, staring up at the top of a silver-tinseled spruce where a blown-glass angel holds aloft a glimmering star. "Tell me that isn't real."

"Smart boy," says Uncle Jack, who at some point has snuck up behind us.

"Thank you, sir," says Hector.

"Glad you found some pants."

"Me too, sir."

Uncle Jack rests a hand on my shoulder. "You think that's something, son, you should see the Sugar Plum Fir inside."

Alice sneaks a look at me. It is not very sneaky, actually. I can tell what she is thinking. It is exactly what Uncle Jack is thinking. They know I haven't been in the Tree Shed since Grampa Chris. And they know I want to go in now. And they want me to know that if I need them, they'll be there for me. Neither of them even has to use their eyebrows to say it.

"I'd like to see it myself," I say. I take Hector's hand. I take Alice's hand too. "Let's go."

The Tree Shed is glorious. A forest of lights. People stop at each tree, marveling at the treasures tucked in its hollows—a paper bird's nest with three small eggs, a glowing spaceship, a glass octopus with a tiny pink mitten on each tentacle—discoverable only by those patient enough to look, there for them alone to find.

Alice and Hector and I walk the picket fence path. We watch the Christmas Express train whir along its tracks, mechanical Santa check his list, Mrs. Claus raise her candle in the imagined dark.

"Looks like you've got a slacker," says Alice. She means the animatronic elf which, unlike the Clauses, is not moving. He is frozen, one hand deep in the plush Santa bag.

"Is he broken?" asks Hector. I don't think he's quite gotten over Rudolph's roadside accident.

"He's okay," I assure him. "Somebody probably forgot to turn him on." I let go of my friends' hands and squat down beside the elf. He's designed to look like he's perched atop a present, but really he's standing on a power box, somewhere on which is a switch. I run my hand around the sides and underneath. I find the switch and something else. Something square and smooth, and even though I have never held it in my own hands, as soon as I touch it I know what it is.

I slip my discovery into my coat pocket. Then I flip the switch and the elf springs to action. He pulls a gift from Santa's pack, hesitates, then shoves it back inside, just as he's done a thousand times before.

"See? He's perfectly fine," I tell Hector, who looks genuinely relieved.

"You seem fine too," Alice whispers to me.

"I am fine," I tell her. "I am more than fine."

She raises an are-you-sure eyebrow.

"Have faith," I tell her. "Have faith."

That night, after the carols are sung and the lights are turned out and Alice and I have hugged goodbye and Hector and I have pretended to find some mistletoe and said good night our own way, my family and I walk down Santa Claus Lane and up the long driveway. We drink cocoa and hang up our stockings like we always do, and Dad reads *The Night Before Christmas* aloud like he always does, and Mom sends Don and Dash and me up to bed like she always does, kissing our foreheads and wishing us sugarplum dreams.

When I get to my room, I shut my door. I turn on the bedside lamp and take from my coat pocket Grampa Chris's small, worn leather notebook. The cover is soft. The pages show proof of the times they've been turned. *Laura's Mom,* it says on the first page. There is no other note. No date. No explanation.

Duncan, it says on the next.

Page after page after page of names. *Greta* and *Steven* and *Varian* and *Mia. Gus* and *Florrie* and *Louie's dog, Clyde.* Each name, a child. Each page, a promise.

Grampa Chris was not checking inventory in the Tree

Shed that day. He wasn't testing the lights, or planning new tree themes, or taking a break from the Summertime Christmas sale. He was keeping his promises. And when his heart stopped and he fell to the ground, I am certain this small leather book fell from his hand and came to rest under that elf. And there it stayed, waiting for the right person to find it. I'll never be able to confirm that, of course, but I don't have to. I can just believe.

Each name, a child. Each page, a promise.

I turn the pages, read the names, until somewhere near the middle of the book, the names stop. The rest of the pages are blank.

I wonder if all these kids got what they most wanted. If their difficult wishes were granted. Or not.

The silver pencil slides easily out of its loop. On the next blank page I write *Olivia*. Then I turn back to the first name in the book. *Laura's Mom*.

I make a promise. To Grampa Chris. To myself. To Laura and Olivia and all the others between. I make a promise.

And then I keep it.

ACKNOWLEDGMENTS

If anything about this book made you love Santa Claus more than you already did, you can thank the folks at the Charles W. Howard Santa Claus School in Midland, Michigan. Never in my life have I been around so many people dedicated to the joy and welfare of children. The weekend I spent there participating in Santa School was magic and I'm forever grateful for what I learned. Reader, if anything in this book makes you feel cynical about what Santas can do, that's on me.

Further thanks go to my Christmas miracle of an editor, Reka Simonsen, who believed in this book from the beginning, and the rest of the Atheneum crew.

Thank you to readers Claire Thompson, Mia Isabella Smith, Kate Messner, Martha Brockenbrough, and Jennifer Zieglar. Excerpts from this book were shared at the Vermont College of Fine Arts, which helped me figure out what was funny and what was just too cringey to include.

Thanks, as always, to the Ladies Sewing Guild for sharing wisdom and encouraging faith.

A weeklong residency at the Vermont Studio Center allowed me the time and focus to draft a large section of this book. If any of you want to give a writer friend a holiday gift, relieve them of the responsibility of making meals for a week. You have no idea what a difference that makes.

Sometimes, my family might have been better off without the meals I did scramble to make. For your patience and support, thank you, Claire, Jack, and, mostly, Julio.